CW01046492

Sleighed

The Coffee House Sleuths

Sleighed

Book 1

T. LOCKHAVEN

EDITED BY:
EMMY ELLIS
GRACE LOCKHAVEN

TWISTED KEY
publishing
2019

First Printing: 2019

ISBN 978-1-947744-39-4

Twisted Key Publishing, LLC
www.twistedkeypublishing.com

Ordering Information:
Special discounts are available on quantity purchases by corporations, associations, educators, and others. For details, contact the publisher at the above listed address.

U.S. trade bookstores and wholesalers: Please contact Twisted Key Publishing, LLC by email twistedkeypublishing@gmail.com.

Contents

Chapter 1

Bitter Sweet Café, Lana Cove, North Carolina

"What's a party without mistletoe?" Michael asked, arching his eyebrows. He savored a sip of pumpkin spice coffee and gazed expectantly across the table at his two best friends.

Ellie and Olivia shared a look that could *only* be interpreted as: *Not this again.*

"I see," Michael deduced. "The silent treatment." He grabbed a napkin from the table and dabbed at the coffee that had dripped from his cup onto his red Christmas sweater, decorated with a tree with flashing lights. Ellie made him turn it off for fear he may cause one of her elderly customers to have a seizure. "When it came to discussing whether our Christmas tree lights should twinkle, you couldn't stop talking. But, I suggest a pristine piece of nature that just *happens* to be intertwined with a time-honored tradition, and suddenly you have nothing to say."

Ellie brushed a fly-away from her forehead, took a sip of coffee and checked her watch. The dinner crowd would be arriving soon.

Olivia licked creamy parfait from her spoon. "I love this song," she sighed. "*Silent Night*, it's so poignant." Ellie nodded in agreement.

Michael leaned in, his blue eyes sparkling mischievously. "Look, mistletoe has virtually *ruined* people's lives, do you realize the power we wield hosting the party at my house? We have the ability to sit back and unleash—"

"Here we go," Ellie complained. "Who *hurt* you as a child?"

"What? No one. I just don't see how you can't see the humor in this. One little sprig hung over a doorway induces equal amounts of anxiety and awkwardness. It's free entertainment." He sat back in his chair and clasped his hands.

"Are you done bloviating?" Ellie asked.

Michael glanced at her, held up a finger, and then wrinkled his forehead. "That depends," he answered cautiously. "I'll need to consult with my thesaurus before answering that... or my attorney—who may also need to consult a thesaurus. It's a vicious circle."

"I'm beginning to understand why you're single," said Ellie.

"Forgive me for having a sense of humor."

"Mistletoe is not funny, Michael West." Olivia brandished her well-licked spoon in his direction.

Ellie put her hand on Olivia's. "Don't, darling. Stay strong. It's not worth it."

Olivia scanned the café, tightened her lips, and then leaned in, whispering furiously, "Do you remember Mary Stewart?"

"The television star that was arrested for insider trading?"

"No," snapped Olivia, "that's Martha Stewart."

"Wasn't she the church secretary at Sacred Heart?" Ellie asked, gently blowing across her coffee.

"Yes," nodded Olivia. "Thank you."

"She's such a sweet old lady," smiled Ellie.

"What does this have to do with our discussion?" inquired Michael, clearly unhappy with the direction the conversation was heading.

"Well, a branch of mistletoe made her do her business behind the bushes at the Weston Country Club—"

"Well, you're not supposed to eat it!" Michael exclaimed. "She's lucky she didn't die."

"She didn't eat it, you buffoon. Father McKenzie thought it would be funny to hang a branch of mistletoe at the entrance to the women's bathrooms."

"Oh my," said Ellie, stifling a giggle. "To get to the restroom, you had to pay the troll."

"Exactly," nodded Olivia. She took in a deep breath, recalling the memory. "He just stood there in the hallway—a twisted smile on his face—waiting with his wintergreen Tic-Tacs. I can still hear the *tap-tap, tap-tap*, as he shook them into his hand—loitering for his next victim." Olivia's voice was barely a whisper.

"Okay…," Michael said. "That took a much darker turn than I expected."

"Ugh." Ellie visibly shuddered. "That's disgusting. He has old man lips. Poor Mrs. Stewart."

Ellie turned and gave Michael a dark look. "I hope you're satisfied, look what you've done to Olivia." She grasped her hand, consoling her.

Michael shook his head. "I'm not really sure what I just witnessed, but you guys have completely deviated from what I was talking about. You've basically vilified a perennial flowering plant by adding a sinister component. What if I replaced Father McKenzie loitering in the hallway with someone like Chris Hemsworth or Paul Rudd? I'm sure things would be *much* different."

"Or Pierce Bronson," a voice piped up from another table.

"He's a looker," agreed a silver-haired woman.

"Not compared to Paul Newman," her friend gushed, "or Steve McQueen. They were real men."

"Yes, they were, Mrs. Taylor," smiled Olivia, who had turned to acknowledge the octogenarians at the table next to theirs.

"You have no idea who any of those people are, do you?"

"Do they predate the internet?" asked Olivia.

"Most likely," said Michael. "Perhaps even the wheel."

"Then no," shrugged Olivia.

"Michael," Ellie tapped his wrist. "I'm simply saying, you can't take a hypothetical and try to merge it with reality," she insisted.

"But I can! Mistletoe is the victim here. Father McKenzie is the wrongdoer!"

"This whole discussion is ridiculous. I mean, really, Michael, if you're so desperate for a kiss from a woman, man up and ask for it."

Michael could feel the blood rush to his face. "I wasn't saying that," he stammered. "Look at me, I can *get* a kiss! I simply wanted to watch—"

There was a gasp and the clanging of silverware from the table behind them. "That is *much* more disturbing on *many* levels," Olivia muttered.

"I agree," nodded Ellie. "Despicable."

"You didn't let me finish." Michael could feel the café's patron's eyes boring into the back of his head. "That was completely out of context—"

"Listen," Ellie interrupted, "I need to make a point, and after this," she insisted, turning to each of her friends, "we are *through* discussing mistletoe, agreed? We *are* adults after all."

Olivia and Michael nodded in unison.

"At least two of us," Olivia sighed under her breath.

"I believe that the mistletoe tradition was created by a sad, sad man named either Lester or Morris," Ellie began. "I'm going to go with Lester—an aficionado of elbow patched sweaters, pleated khakis, and leather shoes with tassels."

"Tassels are hideous," agreed Olivia. "Almost as bad as cufflinks. No respectable woman has ever said, 'I *love* your cufflinks.'"

"Agreed," said Ellie. "The hanging of mistletoe is a pitifully sad, outdated tradition for lonely men who enjoy adolescent humor, juvenile jokes and celibacy."

"Here! Here!" Olivia applauded. "Dramatic yet eloquent. Well done."

"Alright, I'm man enough to admit when I'm defeated." Michael sighed, scooting his chair outside of Ellie's arm's reach. "So, just for clarity... for our holiday party... mistletoe in, or out?"

Michael was saved from certain death when a man's excited voice erupted from the table behind them.

"Turn up the volume! Turn up the volume on the television!" The man shouted at the thirty-something hipster running the cash register.

Ellie and Olivia twisted in their seats to see what the commotion was about. Everyone in the café was staring at the television.

The local news was showing video footage, obviously shot from someone's cell phone. The crawler at the bottom of the screen read: *Lana Cove Mall Mayhem*.

"Oh no." Michael sucked in his breath, frightened there had been a shooting. From the expressions on Olivia's and Ellie's faces, they were thinking the same thing.

The video panned from the floor to Santa, who was seated on a large golden chair with red plush upholstery. Standing to his side was an angelic elf with blonde hair, a green top, red-and-white-striped stockings, and pointy green shoes. A long line of children queued in front of Santa, waiting for their turn.

The videographer was obviously enamored with the elf because his camera zoomed in on her and remained there for some time. It wasn't until she turned with a surprised expression, that the video swooped from her to another man dressed as Santa leaping out from behind the other Santa's chair.

The entire café gasped when the rogue Santa ripped the beard off the seated Santa's face. Then, as if it were a trophy, he thrust the beard into the air and screamed, "He's a fake! He's a fake!"

For a second, the de-bearded Santa didn't seem to know what to do. He glanced around, bewildered. Then he jumped to his feet and chased the other Santa around the stage. The children scattered, screaming, parents rushed forward scooping them in their arms.

The rogue Santa, still clutching the fake beard, crashed through a candy cane barrier and sprinted toward the escalator.

"Is that George?" Ellie asked, horrified. "Please tell me that's not George."

"I'm not sure," Michael said, unable to tear his eyes from the train wreck.

The beardless Santa dove for the rogue, grabbing him by the back of his pants, just as he'd stepped onto the escalator. As fate would have it, Santa's pants dropped to his boots, revealing a pair of silk boxers, tastefully decorated with candy canes.

"Thank God for that," Michael said. "It could have been worse—a lot worse."

The rogue Santa waddled and fell forward onto the escalator. Beardless Santa leaped onto his back. Horrified onlookers gawked and pointed as the literal Santa sandwich slowly ascended, still fighting over the beard.

The news anchor appeared on the screen, a headshot of the rogue Santa behind her shoulder. "It saddens me to say," the woman said in a crisp voice, "a spokesman from the Lana Cove Mall tells us that due to recent events, George Owens will be banned from the mall until further notice."

The atmosphere inside the Bitter Sweet Café immediately shifted from festive to dismay. Whispered conversations filled the room. For many, George was a close, dear friend.

"I don't understand…. Why would he do that?" Ellie asked, her heart breaking for George.

"He wouldn't," Olivia insisted. "This doesn't make any sense."

"It's like he just lost it," Michael replied, bewildered.

"Livs and I have known George for over twenty years. He would never do this," she shook her head. "He's just a sweet old man."

"And who was that other Santa?" Michael asked. "Did either of you recognize him?"

"I don't know," Ellie said, thinking. "I don't think I've ever seen him before. George has been the official Santa at the Lana Cove Mall since before I was born."

"George is pretty old—he may not be able to work as many hours as he used too." Olivia's face dropped. "Why do they have to keep showing that video over and over again? It's like they revel in other people's misery."

"Daryl," Ellie called out to her hipster employee. "Change the channel. Put on anything, I don't care if it's golf."

"I hear George has been tipping it back a little too much lately," a man said a couple tables away.

"Great." Ellie nodded toward the man. "That's how rumors get started. Do you think we should reach out to George and make sure he's okay? He's bound to be devastated."

"Maybe we could invite him to our Christmas party," Olivia offered. "We could use a real Santa. No offense, Michael, you do make a great Santa."

"None taken. I'm always willing to do what needs to be done for the greater good. Besides, I'm dying to try on my new holiday threads, so it's a win-win."

"Actually, I'm pretty sure George is booked up by now," Ellie replied. "He's usually busy from the beginning of December through Christmas."

"I wouldn't be too sure about that." Michael stared at the television. "Take it from someone who's been in marketing his entire life... this is the type of story that goes viral. Trust me." He shook his head. "There's not a lot of people who are going to want an unhinged Santa."

"You're right," Ellie sighed. "I think we should invite him to the party, and if he has a Santa gig, well, that's great. But if not, I'm sure he could use the support of his friends right now."

Chapter 2

In a small town like Lana Cove, bad news traveled fast, and soon, everyone was talking about George. His actions were completely out of character. Many thought he was simply too old and losing his faculties. Whatever the reason, Michael knew that they needed to be there for him.

To George, he wasn't playing the role of Santa, he was everything that embodied Santa. The hopes, the dreams and the magic that came with the holiday—from answering hundreds of letters, visiting the children's hospital, or spending time with the forgotten at the Lana Cove Nursing Home. George had been there for many, filling the emptiness with love and laughter.

Michael knew the feeling of emptiness all too well having moved to Lana Cove from Boston after a bitter divorce tore his family apart. The kind, quirky people of Lana Cove had embraced him as one of their own and Michael had begun to rediscover the man he once was.

He turned his face toward the sky and closed his eyes. Snowflakes fell lazily onto his cheeks, like tiny cold kisses. For a moment, he was back in Boston, his daughter's delicate mittened hand in his, running through the snow, seeing who could catch a snowflake on their tongue—memories of Lexis dragging him to the ground to make snow angels while she giggled uncontrollably. His heart soared at the sound of her laughter, and for that fleeting moment in time, everything was simple, everything was perfect in the world.

The sound of a car passing brought him back to the present.

He breathed in deeply. His daughter, now eighteen, was away in France, traveling with her best friend's family for Christmas. He swallowed hard. This would be his first Christmas without her since his divorce and his new life in Lana Cove. A tear trekked slowly down his face. He stuck out his tongue, catching a snowflake. It melted, just like his heart. What he wouldn't give to relive the past and put family before his career.

A gentle *tap, tap* caught his attention. He glanced toward his house. Ellie stood at the picture window, her face aglow, lit from the candles she placed on the ledge. Michael waved and turned away, embarrassed to be caught in such a private moment.

He'd used the excuse of shoveling the sidewalk to go outside and be alone with his thoughts, but the truth was, it wasn't necessary. A thin dusting of snow like powdered sugar was all that blanketed the walkway and the porch. And with a few whisks from his push broom, he'd cleared the pavement and the porch.

"All right, Michael," he whispered, "get ahold of yourself." He clomped up the porch steps, leaned the broom against the house, kicked the snow off his boots, and stepped inside.

"Welcome back." Ellie smiled. "Beautiful, isn't it?" Her face was pressed to the window, her hands on either side of her head.

"It is," Michael said, talking about Ellie, just as much as he was the snow.

He hung his jacket and scarf in the closet, then removed his snow boots. With the grace of an Olympic skater, he slid sock-footed across the floor and grabbed Ellie's hand. He sang along with Dean Martin as she drew her in and slow danced with her. "In the meadow we can build a snowman, and we'll pretend that he is Parson Brown." She rested her head on his shoulder for a moment, her dark silken hair spilling across his chest, then she turned her head and looked into his eyes. "He'll say are ya married?"

"Well say no, man!" laughed Ellie.

"That was a bit too exuberant."

"Michael," she whispered softly, her brown eyes wide, filled with wonderment.

His heart fluttered. "Yes? *I'll love you forever.*" He was intoxicated by her beauty.

"I'm thinking we put the tree in that corner. That way the guests see it as soon as they enter the room." She smiled, playfully pushing him away.

Michael's heart skipped a beat. His brain had gone to mush. "Wait, what did you say?" This didn't feel at all like the magical moment he'd just envisioned in his mind.

"I said I think the Christmas tree would look much better in that corner."

Michael blinked his eyes and shook his head. "You ruin a beautiful moment because of a tree?"

"Beautiful moment? All I see is an empty corner, and not a lot of time before our guests arrive," she winked at Michael. "Tick-tock, Mr. West," Ellie prompted, tapping an imaginary watch.

"But our moment," Michael sighed. "Plus, how long could it possibly take to put up a Christmas tree?"

"I'll take this question." Olivia walked into the room with three glasses of wine. She handed a glass each to Ellie and Michael. "Do you remember last year?"

"Which part?" Michael asked curiously. "I already apologized for saying your dad looked like a tall Napoleon. I believe I even used the word doppelganger to impress him."

Ellie shook her head, "You can't help yourself, can you?"

"What?" Michael defended himself. "He always had his arm across his chest, with his hand hidden, just like *every* picture of Napoleon. Your father should have been grateful."

"His arm was in a sling, you idiot," Olivia retorted. "Remember he shattered it trying to teach you how to water ski?"

"Oh yeah, I do remember something about him plowing into a dock," Michael replied sheepishly. "So wait, you're still angry about that?"

"No! I was asking if you remembered last year, and what happened regarding your assembly of the tree."

"Hmm." Michael tapped his finger on his chin. "Not really. I seem to remember something about you constantly asking us to try the punch, try the eggnog… and after that it gets a little hazy. I feel like you may have taken advantage of me."

"Hah, don't flatter yourself. Let's just say we found you asleep on the floor, curled around the base of a half-finished tree."

"Oh yeah…," Michael nodded. "I recall some pictures on Facebook. I was wrapped up in silver tinsel with a star attached to my head."

"Good times." Olivia laughed.

"Tell you what," Ellie said, "why don't you set up the tables and put out the dishes. Olivia and I will assemble this beautiful plastic Douglas fir."

"Are you sure?" Michael shrugged. "I mean, aren't men better at assembling things like furniture? Something about spatial awareness."

Ellie narrowed her eyes. "Michael, we're going to pretend like you didn't just say that, and maybe, we'll let you live."

Michael opened his mouth to object but decided against it. "Got it," he mumbled. "Table, dishes, silverware, DJ."

"What was that last part?" Ellie demanded.

"Nothing," Michael called back. He patted his iPhone and smiled, disappearing into the kitchen.

"Ellie, you've checked your watch a dozen times. He'll be here."

"I'm worried about him." Ellie squinted out the window—aside from the porch light and the lamppost at the end of the drive, it was pitch dark outside. "The party starts in thirty minutes, and I really want to talk with George before the guests arrive."

"I'm sure he'll—" Olivia nearly jumped out of her skin when the doorbell rang. "That's probably him now."

Ellie rushed across the room and threw open the door. "George!" she beamed.

"Hi, Ellie." George smiled kindly, brushing the snow from his coat and hat. His eyes appeared tired and sad, his large, bulbous nose and cheeks red from the cold.

"Come in, come in," Ellie gushed. "Did you walk here?" She leaned through the doorway, peering outside for George's bright-red Chrysler Lebaron with wood paneling, made to resemble Santa's sled. "Where's your car? I would have certainly—" she caught herself. "I'm sorry, George, too many questions."

"It's okay, Ellie," he gave her a sad smile. "I understand."

She moved to the side to give him room. He stomped his boots on the welcome mat and then stepped inside.

Ellie's eyes swept over him, a rush of nostalgia filling her mind. *If anyone looks like Santa, it's George.*

"The decorations are beautiful." His voice sounded rough and weary. "You've outdone yourself."

"The decorations are Olivia's handiwork. She's unbelievably talented."

"Hi, George!" Olivia chirped. She wrapped her arms around him. "It's so good to see you. Can I get you a coffee? Punch? Eggnog?"

"Coffee would be nice, thank you, Olivia."

"You got it. I'll add a dash of cinnamon to spice things up a bit," she winked.

Michael appeared in the living room in a pink apron with red piping, the word *Sweet Buns* elegantly embroidered across the front. He followed George's eyes from his face, down to his apron. "It was a gift," he offered. "And," he said defensively, "it's the truth."

George shook his head and laughed. "Does it come with matching slippers?"

"No, but in case I don't get a chance to come sit on your lap, you'll know what I want for

Christmas," Michael teased. "George," he nodded, "it's always good to see you. I've been banished to the kitchen, so I'm gonna get back to my world-famous sausage balls."

Ellie turned to George and shook her head as Michael traipsed back to the kitchen.

"Thank you for inviting me."

"George," she asked delicately, "are you doing okay? We saw that God-awful video on the news, and you've been on our minds ever since."

"I'm all right. Well, I'm not all right, I guess I just feel—"

"Unwanted?" Michael suggested, returning to the room with a pan of sizzling sausage balls.

Ellie gave Michael a what-is-your-problem look and smacked him on the back of the head.

"Sorry," he muttered.

"Well, I was going for betrayed," George's voice caught in his throat. "But I guess unwanted would fit in there just as well, too."

"See?" Michael gestured with a spatula, "He said *unwanted*, so, we're all on the same page."

"Don't you have something to do... in the kitchen, maybe outside?" Olivia said, shooing Michael away.

"He's a strange man," George said thoughtfully.

"Olivia and I prefer to call him... unique."

"He's a work in progress, like most men." Olivia laughed, scrunching up her nose.

"So," Ellie prompted, "the guests are going to be here soon. What can we do to help?"

George's gaze fell to the floor. "I've been thinking about all of this drama. I'm getting old. Maybe it's just my time, Ellie. I've never blown up like that before. It was shameful." He shook his head. "Just shameful. I've been Santa here in Lana Cove for over forty years, before you two were even born."

"And you still are, to me, to Olivia, to the people here in Lana Cove. Why would you say that it's your time? You know that's not true."

"You bring so much happiness and joy to people's lives."

"Then why would they fire me from the mall after all these years? And now," he set his jaw, "my reputation is ruined. You know how this world is, Ellie—everything is perception. They don't even care about reality or the truth anymore."

A loud *bang* followed by a *gasp* came from the kitchen. The group paused their conversation as a series of high-pitched *beeps* chimed in.

"Excuse me," said Olivia with a sigh, "I better check on that."

Ellie waited as her friend scurried away and then turned her attention back to George. "Aside from the video, did something happen at the mall? I mean what possible reason would they have for firing you?"

"Absolutely nothing!" George reddened from his outburst. "I'm sorry, this whole thing has got me so worked up."

"It's okay," said Ellie soothingly. "I'm just trying to see if there was some horrible misunderstanding."

"No, it came out of the blue. I was on my way to work, when I received a call from Ed Reed's secretary telling me I was fired. A phone call! They didn't even have the decency to tell me to my face."

"I'm so sorry," was all Ellie could muster, her mind searching for the right words to say, the right questions to ask.

"And, as if that wasn't the worst of it," George continued, "ever since that horrid video of me came out, several of my biggest clients cancelled on me. I even lost the Bernstein account."

"Oh, that's horrible." Ellie felt like the wind had been knocked out of her.

The Bernstein Gala was an incredible annual event held at the Bernstein Mansion. A multi-million-dollar oceanfront estate that had been featured on the *Travel Channel* and *The Homes of the Rich and Famous* series. Last Christmas, Barry Manilow had entertained guests at the party. Every year, the Bernsteins held a raffle, and twenty-five families were invited from around Lana Cove to come feast and celebrate Christmas. George had been a part of the celebration for the past twenty years.

"Robert… Mr. Bernstein," George clarified, "told me that the recent events on television would tarnish his reputation. He didn't want anything to ruin the pristine perception of his perfect party. So he hired the new Santa… Drew Small."

"Drew Small?" Ellie thought for a moment. "I've never heard of him. He looked a little young to be Mr. Reed's choice for a new Santa."

"He doesn't even have a real beard!" George exclaimed. "But," embarrassment shown red on his cheeks, "you already know that."

"Yeah." Ellie smiled affectionately. "So, you have no idea who this guy is or why Mr. Reed would have hired him?"

"None, and believe me, I checked. He's not a member of the official Santa union, and he's not a member of the official Santa's Facebook page or the North Pole Answering Service."

"North Pole Answering Service?" Ellie enquired.

"The local post office brings children's letters—addressed to Santa—to me, and I answer them," George explained.

"That's really sweet. I had no idea that was even a thing."

"What's really sweet?" Olivia asked, balancing two trays of holiday cookies on her arms. "Don't say it, Michael," she yelled toward the kitchen.

"He was going to say *you are*, wasn't he?" George asked.

"If you look up predictable in the dictionary…."

"You'll find his picture." Ellie sighed.

"Guilty." Michael laughed, stepping into the living room, wiping his hands on his apron.

"George was telling me…," she paused and turned to George to make sure it was okay to continue. He nodded and gestured for her to keep going. "…that a man named Drew Small took his job at the mall and the Bernstein Estate."

"Drew Small," Michael chuckled. "He's just lucky his first name isn't Richard." He glanced expectantly from Ellie to George to Olivia. "Not funny?"

"Not in the slightest," Ellie replied.

"Fine, how about the name Drew Small, sounds like someone who specializes in miniature works of art. A gunslinger with tiny pistols? Nothing? Oh come on."

"Currently he's specializing in making George's life miserable," Ellie chided, "and you're not helping."

"I'm belittling him, that's gotta be somewhat helpful."

Ellie arched an eyebrow and crossed her arms.

"Fine, while I was in the kitchen, I was actually multi-tasking," said Michael defensively.

"Yes, we *heard*."

"George, you said Ed Reed's secretary called and gave you the news, correct?" George responded with a nod, knowing that there was more to come. "Did you try to get in touch with Mr. Reed personally, I mean you two are friends, right?"

"Of course. Ed's an incredibly busy man. He's in charge of all the special events around the city. He and I have worked together on the Santa extravaganza for years. I've tried calling. I've left messages. I've texted him. This isn't like him. I honestly don't know what happened."

"Were there any complaints? Any angry parents? Anything that would cause them to fire you?" Ellie inquired delicately.

"Nothing. I never heard so much as a peep of anyone being upset. I woke up Thursday morning, got dressed to go to the mall—and that's when I got the phone call, letting me know I'd been fired. I knew there had to be some kind of mistake. I tried to get Ed on the phone, but it kept going to his voicemail, so I headed to the mall to figure out what had happened."

"So, you were never able to talk to Ed in person?" Ellie prompted.

"No. That was the craziest part. Ellie, you don't just fire someone after forty years. I went to Ed's office, but Jan, his secretary, told me he wasn't there. I knew he was there. I could see a light under his door, and I saw his shadow under the doorway. Ed was there…."

"Okay, so Ed wouldn't talk to you, then what did you do?" Michael asked.

"Well, I figured if Ed wasn't going to talk to me, I would try to talk to the new Santa, you know, maybe he would be nice enough to at least tell me what was going on."

"Okay." Ellie nodded. "Go on."

"So…." George's face turned red. "I went to the men's restroom, across from the employee breakroom. I figured he'd have to come there and change. We weren't allowed to wear our Santa suit outside the mall. You don't want a child to see you exiting your car in your Santa outfit," he explained. "Imagine my surprise when this kid in his thirties comes in and dumps his Santa suit out onto the bathroom floor from a black trash bag. The disrespect..." he huffed. "He would have been kicked out of the NSU instantly. National Santa Union," he clarified. "That *suit*," George emphasized, "is sacred, and it's an *honor* to wear it."

"Completely understood," Ellie nodded again. "And you confronted Drew?"

"Well, not so much confronted him. I asked him how he got the job, and he told me to mind my own business."

"Did he know who you were?" asked Michael.

"No, not until I told him. I let him know that I was the original Santa and that I'd been fired. I told him I just wanted to know why I'd been replaced. So instead of being a decent human being, the kid laughed in my face and told me to stop harassing him or he'd call security."

"Let me guess," Michael said, "you tried to reason with him."

"I asked him again, *nicely*, if he had any idea why I was fired. He got all angry and said something like 'Suit yourself, old man.' He threw his trash bag to the floor and stormed out of the restroom. Next thing I know, two security guards showed up and asked me to leave, like I was a criminal or something."

"Only you didn't," Michael prodded gently.

"No. I know I should have… but as you know, hindsight is twenty-twenty."

"I couldn't agree more," said Michael.

"So, I went to my car and sat there. I should have left." George shook his head. "Because the longer I sat there, the angrier I got. Finally, I couldn't take it anymore, I just needed some answers, so I snuck in through the employee entrance, made my way to the winter wonderland set—the set that *I* created— and when I saw him sitting there in my chair, and his fake beard… I just lost it… I wasn't trying to hurt the guy." George stared at the floor. "The rest, well, you've seen the video. After that, I was escorted out and banned from the mall."

"That's a bit much," Olivia said, angrily shaking her head.

"You devote so much of your life… and in the blink of an eye, it's taken away from you," Ellie complained.

"Seems like ripping a beard off a person, parading around and waving it in the air like it's your enemy's head is frowned upon," George said.

"Ellie, you, Olivia, and George have lived here in Lana Cove for eons. George, you grew up here, and you're like a hundred years old—"

Ellie flashed an annoyed look at Michael.

"Okay, fine, ninety," Michael apologized. "My question is, do *any* of you know if there is a family of Smalls living in Lana Cove?"

The group immediately shook their heads in unison.

"I'm just a bit confused."

"You're just now admitting it," muttered Olivia.

"This young guy shows up to a small town and starts taking all the Santa gigs and besmirching our friend? No one sees this as being odd?" asked Michael.

"Yes and no, a huge part of our community is made up of transplants. You showed up and said you quit your job in Boston, and gave up everything to become a mystery writer, and no one thought that was strange," Olivia pointed out.

"Well, of course not, look at me, I am the literal personification of a successful writer, so not too much of a stretch there. Plus, my job doesn't require me to dress up as a fictional character, and it doesn't only pay one month out of a year."

"True." Olivia bobbed her head. "Yours pays in imaginary money—from the future."

"That's a fair assessment," Michael agreed. "All I'm trying to say is, we need to find out who he's connected with here, and why he's actually here. Why would Mr. Reed suddenly fire Michael and give a thirty-something the job of Santa? The plot thickens."

"Unlike your hair," smiled Olivia.

"I hate to say it," Ellie choked on her words, "but Michael's right."

Michael nearly dropped his sugar cookie. "One moment," he fished his phone out of his pocket and pressed record. "Could you please repeat the part where you said Michael is right? Feel free to add any embellishments you deem necessary."

"I'm just agreeing that things don't add up." She pushed Michael's phone away and turned her attention back to George. "We'll try to get this all sorted out in the morning. Emotions are running high tonight."

"I agree," said George.

"We'll start by seeing if Drew has any family here, and then go from there. Let's try to have a good night and we'll get a fresh start on things in the morning," smiled Ellie kindly.

A pair of headlights flashed in the picture window, and then another. "That's my cue,"

George said. "Where would you like me to change?"

"In the guest bedroom," Michael responded. "It's the second door on the right. There's a bathroom in there, and a treadmill should you get the urge to work off a few pounds."

"George." Ellie placed her hand gently on his arm as he turned to leave. "I want you to remember that you are surrounded by friends and people who love you. I promise you, tomorrow will be better."

"Thank you, Ellie… and you too, Olivia." George smiled affectionately.

"What about me?" Michael asked, clearly feeling left out.

"Two lumps of coal for you." George laughed as he disappeared down the hallway to get ready. "Two lumps of coal."

"I like him." Michael grinned. "A consummate professional, already in character."

"Two lumps of coal," George's voice rang out again from the guest room.

Chapter 3

It was the perfect night for a Christmas party. A steady snow had begun to fall, covering Lana Cove under a pristine, cottony blanket of white. Olivia had transformed Michael's living room into a Christmas work of art—candles flickering in the windows, a rainbow of lights twinkling on the Christmas tree. The faux fireplace was adorned with stockings, and old-fashioned lanterns glowed on either side of the hearth.

Olivia had just finished lighting candles on the beautifully decorated table when the doorbell rang.

"I'll get it," Ellie chirped as she opened the door for the newly arrived guests. "Andrew, Denise." She gave them each a kiss on the cheek. "Come in, come in. I *love* that houndstooth jacket," she gushed. "It's gorgeous."

"Thank you, Ellie. Hi, Michael," Denise said, waving.

Ellie moved aside and turned her head toward Michael. "Oh God," she gasped.

"What?" Michael asked innocently, proudly sporting a bright-red Christmas sweater adorned with flashing colorful lights, green pants, and white patent-leather shoes. He wasn't sure, but he swore envy filled Andrew's eyes.

"Michael," Ellie stammered, "what are you wearing? It's…it's…."

"Breathtaking?" Michael prompted. "Exquisite?"

"Abysmal," she groaned.

"What are you talking about, El? He looks dashing," Andrew replied, winking at Michael.

"See?" Michael gloated, empowered by Andrew's comments. He plucked a curly pipe from his pocket and tapped it on his pants leg. "What?" He shrugged at Ellie's look of disdain. "It's not a *real* pipe. It just adds an air of sophistication to—"

"Is that George's pipe?" Olivia demanded.

"No." Michael stared at her indignantly. "Okay, fine, I may have inadvertently removed it from his jacket when I gave him a hug. You should be thankful—I may be saving his life."

"You're incorrigible," Ellie cried. "Why can't you dress like Andrew? Look at him: Burberry scarf, beautiful gray coat, black slacks. It's like he just stepped out of a *GQ* photo shoot."

Andrew tugged up his pants leg, revealing a bright-red pair of socks with reindeer. A mischievous, childlike grin filled his face.

"Well," Olivia checked out Andrew's socks, "they are both festive and tasteful."

"Don't forget to add whimsical," Andrew piped in.

"Your outfit," she said, facing Michael, "well, there aren't any words."

"Your jealousy is palatable. As the great artist Julliard Dasani once said, 'Pure beauty is indescribable,'" Michael retorted.

"It's going to be a long night," sighed Olivia.

🎄🎄🎄🎄

The living room bubbled with conversation and laughter. There was something about Christmas music that made people happy. A rollicking game of Secret Santa found Michael relinquishing his sweater in exchange for Andrew's reindeer socks. Michael considered himself the victor—he had all but lusted over Andrew's finery.

As the adults settled down, clustered in tiny groups, Olivia grabbed a glass and pinged it with a fork. She smiled, seemingly a little embarrassed by the sudden attention. "Well!" she laughed. "That was a lot more effective than I thought it would be." She glanced around the room, addressing the children. "We have a special guest tonight."

The children stared at her with rapt attention.

"Who?" Cindy asked, a little brown-haired, brown-eyed girl, incredibly adorable in her plush green-and-silver dress.

Olivia nodded at Michael. The children let out a chorus of dejected moans when they saw him.

"No, no, no, not him, someone *special*," Olivia said, laughing.

Michael played the first notes of *Santa Claus is Comin' to Town* on his piano.

The children's eyes flew open wide, and Cindy held her hand over her mouth, barely covering her *Oh!* expression.

"Is it Santa Claus?" she whispered shyly.

Olivia couldn't take it—the little girl was just too cute. "I think so!"

Cindy threw her hands together and jumped up and down as Michael played the song.

George's voice rang through the house. "Ho-ho-ho!"

And when he appeared in the living room, the children gasped in unison. "Santa!"

Ellie glanced at Olivia. All of her childhood memories came flooding back to her. Just about every person in the room had visited George for Christmas. If there ever was a Santa… it was George.

The children danced around his legs and hugged him—their faces filled with pure delight. George's blue eyes twinkled, filled with magic. He took a seat in front of the fireplace and removed a beautifully illustrated *The Night Before Christmas* book from his satchel. The children sat on the floor at his feet, as he read the story. Not a creature was stirring, not even a mouse.

When he was finished, George closed the book and smiled at the children. He leaned forward. The children scooched closer—they couldn't take their eyes off him. "I've got a gift for each of you. Now remember," he said softly, "Christmas isn't for a couple more days, but since all of you have been so good this year… well, except for Michael," he winked. He held his hand up to his mouth and whispered, "He's on my naughty list."

The children gasped, and adults broke into laughter.

"Maybe if he tries really hard over the next couple days," Santa joked playfully, "I'll have the elves make him something."

The children nodded in agreement. A small boy crossed his arms and added, "*If* he behaves."

George reached into his satchel and gave each child a candy cane and a gift, wrapped in silver paper with a blue ribbon.

"And for the parents, so you can start a tradition with your children...." He handed each of the adults an illustrated copy of *The Night Before Christmas*.

Cindy looked at her gift and then at Michael. She turned and whispered something quietly in Santa's ear. He nodded and dug in his bag, handing her another copy of the book. Cindy proudly marched over to Michael and gave it to him.

"What's this?" asked Michael. Cindy pulled on Michael's shoulder, and he leaned in toward her.

"I told Santa that everyone needs something special on Christmas," she said quietly.

Her voice tickled Michael's ear, and for a moment he disappeared back to that place, when his daughter held his hand and whispered in his ear. The words tickling both his ear and his heart.

"Thank you." Michael hugged Cindy. "Thank you so much."

"Try to be good, okay?" Cindy said as she walked away. Michael swallowed a lump in his throat.

George caught Ellie's eye. He mouthed *thank you* and then bid farewell to everyone as *I'll Be Home for Christmas* began to play.

Chapter 4

Olivia stretched and rubbed her hands across her legs. Her bright-red nose matched her fuzzy earmuffs. "It's brutal out there."

"It's thirty-one, practically a spring day in Boston," Michael winked. He took a bite of his egg-and-cheese croissant and flipped open his laptop. "Supposed to snow until this evening." He wiped his mouth off on his sleeve.

"You're such a Neanderthal," Olivia chided, sliding a napkin over to him.

"Hey, don't disparage Neanderthals." Ellie laughed. She wrapped her fingers around her coffee mug for warmth. "So, what's the plan? Livs and I have to work until three."

"You own the café… can't you give yourself a break? What about the millennial?" Michael tilted his head toward the pale, thin male in a white button-down shirt and black skinny jeans. "Can't he stay a little later?"

"He pulled a double yesterday. He said he has to have time to go to Soul Cycle and then do some Christmas shopping for his family."

"Soul Cycle? He's so thin he could wear my watch as a belt."

"Leave Dwayne alone. He's a sweetie and a hard worker. Trust me, those are difficult to come by nowadays."

"I can imagine," Michael agreed. "Okay, while you and Olivia are prodding your customers for clues, I'll swing by the mall. Hopefully I'll be able to find out a bit more about Drew."

"All right," Ellie nodded. "Give us a buzz if you discover anything. We'll do the same." Michael was about to stand when Ellie grabbed him by the arm. "Don't do anything stupid, okay?" she smiled playfully at him. "I spent all my bail money on presents."

"I appreciate your heartfelt concern. I'll do my best to stay out of trouble," Michael promised as he polished off the last of his croissant.

🎄🎄🎄🎄

Michael eased off of the A1A highway onto Mall Drive. For a smallish-sized town, the Lana Cove

Mall was a cornucopia of big-name department stores as well as boutique shops that catered to the more sophisticated connoisseur—the type of patron who wouldn't think twice about dropping a couple hundred dollars on scented candles with names like 'vanilla pumpkin spice' or 'cinnamon latte.'

Michael eased his red Miata into the mall parking lot. It was a lightweight car and didn't handle well in the snow. He drove along the outer loop and parked at the back of the Macy's department store. The yearly Santa Extravaganza was hosted by Macy's, so it made sense to Michael that Drew would park at the back entrance.

He took a sip of his hazelnut coffee and flicked his wipers twice, clearing the snow off his windshield. Bright-orange plows, their amber lights flashing, were busy creating mountains of snow. An older woman clambered out of her car, one arm wrapped tightly around her coat, the other clutching her hat. The wind had picked up, gusting across the parking lot. Her scarf danced behind her like the tail of a kite. Christmas wreaths with red ornaments swung back and forth, clanging on the light posts.

A steady stream of employees arrived, leaning against the wind, slipping and sliding as they made their way into Macy's back entrance. Michael grabbed a blueberry bagel from his bag and flicked the windshield wipers again. A metallic-blue Honda Accord pulled into a parking space facing him, a few cars to his left. He stopped chewing and leaned forward.

There was quite a bit of commotion in the front seat of the Honda. The windshield of Michael's car was beginning to fog up. Using his sleeve, he cleared a small circle so he could watch. The driver side door of the Honda popped open and a man in jeans and a black jacket hopped out. He opened the back door and tugged out a black trash bag.

"That must be Drew," Michael whispered to himself. *I see he hasn't upgraded his luggage*, he referred to the black bag where George had told them Drew kept his Santa suit.

A woman in a puffy white coat and brown leggings joined him. She looked like a marshmallow on a stick.

Michael grabbed his phone and fired off a quick text to Ellie. A few moments later, the words *I can't afford bail* appeared on his phone, with an emoji of a bag of money.

He rolled his eyes and watched Drew and the marshmallow lady disappear inside the mall. *I'll give them five minutes. Just enough time to finish my coffee and bagel*, he told himself, brushing crumbs from his lap.

He took one final sip of coffee, checked his surroundings and then gently pushed his car door open. A gust of wind buffeted the car, slamming the door on his leg.

"Mother Mary," Michael gasped, yanking his leg back inside. He raised his knee against his chest and sat for a long while, rocking. Finally, after the pain had abated, he cinched up his pants leg, quite certain the only thing that had kept him from severing his foot were the festival holiday reindeer socks he had won from Andrew at the Christmas party.

Assured that he would indeed walk again, he studied himself in the rearview mirror and adjusted his black baseball cap, drawing it low on his forehead. He narrowed his eyes. He had to admit, he was ruggedly handsome. Michael shoved the car door open, stepping lithely to the side. Just as he praised his athleticism, another gust of wind tore his baseball cap from his head, sending it skittering across the parking lot.

Michael sighed, watching his favorite cap disappear beneath a row of cars. He quickly limped across the parking lot to Drew's car, wincing with every step.

The first thing Michael spotted was the barcode on the back window. *Rental car.* He moved to the rear and fished out his phone. *Florida plates.* He swiped to his photo app and snapped a picture of the license plate and barcode.

I wonder if…. He tried the handle of the passenger door. *Locked.* He tried the driver and passenger doors, all locked. Of course it wouldn't be that easy. He held his phone to his face, as if making a phone call, and scanned the parking lot. With the wind and the snow, it was nearly impossible to see anything.

Satisfied he wasn't being observed, Michael reached inside his pocket and removed an air wedge bag—a small inflatable black bag about the size of a plastic sandwich bag. It was connected to a thin tube with an egg-shaped inflator attached at the end. It worked like a miniature bicycle pump. He carefully inserted the edge of the bag between the door and the doorframe and inflated it.

He removed a thin rod—that looked like a collapsible pointer with a rubber tip—from his pocket and poked it inside the space created by the inflatable bag. He then maneuvered the stick south, until it hovered just above the door's unlock button. He pressed downward, and a satisfying metallic click sounded as the door released.

Like a pro, Michael smiled. He quickly removed the inflator and collapsible rod, pocketed them and slipped into the passenger's side of Drew's car. Settling into the cold vinyl seat, he opened the glove box. It was nearly empty except for the owner's manual and, the coup de grâce, the Hertz rental agreement.

Well hello, Mr. Calvetti. He pulled out his phone and took pictures of the rental agreement. Michael opened the center console—it was filled with gum and candy bar wrappers.

"What's this?" Michael flipped over a circular card with a hook at the top, meant to be hung from the rearview mirror. "Parking pass for the Beach Comber Motel," he flipped it over. "Issued on November 12th. Mr. Calvetti, it looks like you've been here a while."

Michael quickly checked beneath the driver's and passenger seats but didn't find anything of interest. He wedged his hand between the console and the seat, his fingers brushed against something that felt like a napkin or a tissue. Michael closed his eyes—this certainly wasn't the glamorous part of detective work. He shifted in his seat, wiggling his fingers. "Gotcha!" He was rewarded with a black bowtie.

Why would Calvetti need a black bowtie? Michael examined the stained clip-on and slipped it into his jacket pocket.

He located the trunk release and pulled the lever popping it open. Michael made his way to the back of the car. Just as he lifted the trunk and gazed inside, a gust of wind ripped it from his hand, slamming it shut like a gunshot.

Surprised, Michael jumped back, his feet slipping on the slick pavement. He fell back onto the hood of the car parked behind him. He righted himself, thankful that the car he'd fallen on didn't have an alarm. He was contemplating breaking into Drew's car again when the flashing light of a security truck caught his attention. Michael hurried back to his car as it rounded the corner. He pushed the ignition button and flicked on his seat warmers as the security truck slowly made its way between the row of cars.

Michael was shaking. Adrenaline coursed through his body. With shaky fingers, he fished his phone from his jacket pocket, swiped his thumb across the screen and tapped on Ellie's name. She picked up on the third ring.

"Well, your call isn't coming from a payphone, so I'm guessing you're not in jail."

"Sorry to disappoint. I can hear the concern in your voice, and I gotta tell you, it's heartwarming."

"So. Whaddya got? We're slammed."

"A few things," Michael replied as the commotion of the café filtered through his phone. "First, his name is actually Drew *Calvetti*."

"Calvetti," she repeated. "That name sounds so familiar…. It'll come to me."

"I'm pretty sure you wouldn't know him—he listed a Virginia address and phone number."

"I don't know if I would trust that. He could be using a stolen identity."

"Yeah, I'll run a background check on him when I get back to my house. I also found out that he's staying at the Beach Comber Motel. He's been there since the middle of November."

"The Beach Comber… that's actually a great place to stay if you're trying to fly under the radar. It's a cash-only establishment if you get my drift."

"Hmm, interesting… you know so much about it. Almost like—"

"I've never stayed there," Ellie sighed. "I've lived here my whole life. Wait, why am I explaining myself to you?"

"I don't know, guilty conscience? I do have one of those faces where people love to tell me their deepest, darkest secrets. Anything else you'd care to divulge?"

"You wish. Okay, so that pretty much confirms our assumption that he isn't a local."

"Agreed. Did you and Livs find out anything?"

"Not really anything we didn't already know after talking to George. I'll let you know if we find out anything substantial after the lunch rush."

"Alright," said Michael, flicking on his lights and windshield wipers. "I'm going to head home and see what I can dig up on the mysterious Drew Calvetti."

"Good luck!"

"You, too." Michael ended the call and pulled out of the parking lot onto Mall Drive, anxious to discover the true identity of the man behind the fake beard.

Chapter 5

Ellie, Olivia, and Michael followed the hostess to a tall table at the back of Rumor's Bar and Grill—a beachside upscale restaurant frequented by Lana Cove locals. A jazz band set the mood, playing light and bouncy renditions of holiday favorites, punctuated with a thumping baseline.

"Wow!" Olivia exclaimed, gesturing toward the band dressed in red blazers, gold shimmering ties, and green pants, "they're really good."

"Yeah," Ellie said. "I love those upright basses, such a unique rich sound."

"And that pianist," said Michael, helping the ladies as they shrugged out of their winter coats, "he's amazing."

A young Asian woman in a white button-down shirt and black skirt arrived at their table. "Hello, everyone. I'm Jen, I'll be your server tonight. May

I interest you in a cocktail, or perhaps an appetizer?"

"It's a cold, wintery night," Ellie mused. "I think I'll have a Moscow Mule."

"Nice," Olivia replied, "make that two."

"And you, sir?"

"I'll take an Old Fashioned, with Maker's Mark."

"Would you like a sweater vest with that and some reading glasses?" Ellie teased.

"Funny. The Old Fashioned is a classic."

"So is *Gone with the Wind*," smiled Ellie.

"The truth is, Jen," Michael sighed as he gestured toward Ellie and Olivia, "they fight over me constantly. Honestly, it's embarrassing. I told them, it's Christmas, just put a big red bow on me, and—"

"And… I think I just lost my appetite," Ellie groaned.

"I'll be right back with your drinks," Jen smiled politely.

"You really think she's coming back?" asked Olivia.

"Would you?" laughed Ellie.

"You two are quite the team." Ellie and Olivia beamed back at him with satisfaction in their eyes.

"So, aside from maligning my choice of drink, do you have any news about George or Drew?"

"A smidgen," said Ellie. "However, I *may* be reaching here...."

Michael arched his eyebrows. "What did you find out?" He leaned forward on his elbows.

"You said that Calvetti came here, to Lana Cove around Thanksgiving, right?"

"A week or so before Thanksgiving, yes."

"Well, here's where I may be reaching. You know Mrs. Mallory?"

"I don't think... so," Michael furrowed his brow.

"She was a professional golfer about twenty years ago. A wing of the country club is named after her," Ellie explained, giving the story some much-needed context.

"Oh," Michael snapped his finger. "*That* Mrs. Mallory. Yes," he gestured for Ellie to continue.

"She was recently robbed. The thief stole a seventy-thousand-dollar diamond necklace from her house."

Michael let out a low whistle. "That's a nice necklace. And you think it was Calvetti?"

"The timeline makes sense," offered Olivia.

"I don't know," said Michael. "I don't see Drew stealing an expensive necklace and then taking a low paying Santa gig after a heist. If I were him, I would get out of town." He shook his head. "What did the police say?"

"According to Mr. Cole, our source—"

"And town gossip," Olivia added.

"Yes," Ellie agreed. "He said that there was no sign of a break-in or forced entry. Mrs. Mallory's not even sure *when* it went missing."

Michael's brow furrowed again. "Not sure when it went missing?"

"It's not that surprising. An exquisite piece like that, you only wear to social events. It's not everyday jewelry."

"And the only reason she found out that it was missing was because she had planned a trip to Italy, and she kept her passport in the safe with her valuables," explained Olivia.

Michael rubbed his day-old stubble with the side of his hand. "We can assume that she has a sophisticated alarm system. I've seen her house, it's like a fortress. And, I'm sure she has a top of the line safe."

"Yes," said Olivia. "No forced entry. The safe wasn't damaged. The alarm was never triggered."

"Which makes sense," said Michael. "If you're having guests over or a dinner party, you're going to have your alarm system unarmed. If the safe wasn't damaged, we can assume that she left it unlocked."

"Mrs. Mallory is kind of like royalty here, in certain circles. After sixty years of living here, I'm sure that being robbed at one of her social events never crossed her mind."

"It's never a problem until it's a problem," Michael declared sagely.

"You get that off a cereal box?" Olivia teased.

"No, from Mr. Lambert, my psychology professor. He said people find safety through repetition and routines. Unfortunately, routines establish a predictable pattern which can be exploited."

"Jeesh, Michael," Ellie winked. "You actually sounded smart for a minute. Try not to make that a habit."

"Yeah," agreed Olivia, making a face. "It doesn't suit you."

"I'll try not to make it a habit. I'm just saying my professor may have been right. I was rereading a lecture about a renowned jewelry thief for my book—"

"Speaking of books, don't forget you promised to pay for my master's degree with your royalties," interrupted Olivia.

"Good luck," muttered Ellie under her breath.

"Anyways, for those of you still interested in *knowledge*," Michael continued. "My psych professor said most of his victims had a false sense of security established by their environment: gated community, high-rise apartment, comfortable routines. He would find thousands of dollars' worth of jewelry simply laying out in the open."

"I can relate. I can't tell you how many times I've gone to sleep with my windows open and my door unlocked. What…? I just feel safe here," Olivia shrugged, seeing Ellie's look of disapproval.

"Don't say that too loud," whispered Ellie. "You never know who's listening." Her eyes roamed around the room as she spoke.

"Did the police have suspects? Anything to go on?" Michael asked.

"Not really," said Ellie. "It's difficult without a timeline and Mrs. Mallory has a very busy social life. She spent this summer in England, she hosts a weekly book club, and *now* she hosts afternoon tea and biscuits with her close friends."

"And don't forget her annual Thanksgiving and Christmas party."

"That's a lot of opportunity," Michael said.

"And with so many people having access to her house…." Ellie spread her hands as if laying out her cards.

"Have you ever been to one of her Thanksgiving events?" asked Michael.

"We put a bid in to do catering for her, however, we weren't refined enough. Her shindigs are usually black-tie affairs, and we didn't have the necessary equipment to fulfill her menu requests."

"Makes sense, I'm sure she had quite the eclectic menu," said Michael.

Ellie narrowed her eyes. "You're holding out on us."

"No, not at all. When you said black-tie, you reminded me of this," he reached into his pocket and placed the clip-on bowtie on the table.

Ellie picked up the bowtie and examined it. "Even if this is Drew's, it doesn't place him at Mrs. Mallory's house."

"No, but I don't believe in coincidences, especially when it comes to a criminal with a rap sheet as long as my arm," said Michael.

"That's right, you were running a background check on Drew, did you discover anything?"

"Hmm," said Olivia, sounding surprised. "I didn't even know you knew how to do that."

"I don't, but a friend of mine in human resources at my old company owed me a couple favors. She actually ran the report for me."

"So," said Olivia excitedly. "Spill!"

"Mr. Calvetti has quite an extensive record. He's done time for assault, burglary, grand theft auto, bank fraud, and… from the court records I found, he has ties to the Calvetti crime family."

"That's where I know the name Calvetti!" exclaimed Ellie. "Are you sure we're talking about the same guy?"

"Yes, my friend forwarded mug shots from his past two convictions—it's him. I just don't know why he's still around."

"I don't know either, but he seems pretty dangerous to me. Assault charges…," Ellie shook her head. "George is lucky he didn't get hurt."

"So, all we've got to do is let Mr. Reed know that his new Santa isn't so *jolly* after all and get George his job back."

"Ahem," Michael cleared his throat, looking uncomfortable. "I know that's what we all want to do, Livs, but… just hear me out for a moment. I feel like there is something much bigger at play here."

From the look on Ellie's lips tightening into a thin line, she didn't seem too fond of Michael's opinion. "I'm listening."

Michael nodded and continued. "When I first found out about Calvetti's criminal record, I thought he was just trying to lay low and make some cash. I mean, where better than Lana Cove to disappear for a while? But then you tell me about the necklace—why not just sell the necklace and disappear?"

Michael paused when Jen arrived at the table. She leaned between Ellie and Olivia, placing the copper cups onto the table. She smiled at Michael and placed his Old Fashioned onto a black napkin.

"I'll be right back to take your orders," said Jen in a singsong voice.

"Where was I? Oh yes, pawning off the necklace. Drew doesn't leave, he sticks around for a menial job—no disrespect to George—and then he gets into a public confrontation that's televised. It doesn't make sense."

"So what are you suggesting?" asked Ellie, taking a sip of her drink.

"I want George to get his job back more than anything, but I think Drew is up to something, and if we spook him too badly… he'll disappear."

"It would certainly help if we could put him at Mrs. Mallory's house. Then we'd pretty much know that it was him who stole the necklace," said Olivia.

"Of course. It also becomes more problematic if he did. It means there *is* something greater than a seventy-thousand-dollar necklace involved. It doesn't make sense that he would just hang around waiting to get caught."

Ellie traced her finger around the rim of her drink. "Maybe the theft of the necklace was simply an opportunity that presented itself."

"Perhaps he was there to mix and mingle with the wealthy," Olivia suggested. "Like you said, there are a lot of rich people that attend Mrs. Mallory's social events."

"Right now all we can do is guess. You guys said you put a bid with other vendors to cater her party. Is there a way to get a list of the other caterers? Maybe the person in charge would recognize him."

"We can try," said Ellie. "We're friendly with most of the local owners."

"Alright," smiled Jen, returning to the table. "I'll start with the ladies." Ellie ordered the sea bass with capers and lemon garlic butter. Olivia opted for grilled chicken breast with broccoli and Yukon potatoes, and Michael chose a Caesar salad with grilled chicken.

"Oh, and no anchovies," he called out to Jen as she walked away.

"I wonder," said Ellie, thinking aloud, "if there is actually a Drew Small."

"You can bet your bottom dollar there is," said Michael. "Think about it. You know the mall is going to run a background check on the person they hire for Santa, and I'm sure Mr. Bernstein's estate performs extensive checks on all their employees."

"Maybe he's here trying to start his life over," suggested Olivia. "And it's just circumstantial that the necklace vanished at the same time."

"I don't know about that," said Michael.

"A lot of people move to small towns and try to blend in. He only got confrontational when George began asking questions, and then ripped his beard off and embarrassed him in public."

Ellie shook her head. "Drew appears in November and Mrs. Mallory's necklace is stolen. Then, George is suddenly fired, and who takes his place? Drew."

"Then we find out that he's using a false identity," added Michael, "and he has an extensive criminal record."

"Excuse me," Jen's presence surprised everyone at the table. "I apologize for interrupting, but are you Michael West?"

"Yes I am," said Michael, puffing up his chest. He gave Jen a broad smile. "My book isn't even published yet, and I'm already being recognized in public." Olivia and Ellie sighed in unison.

Michael took the piece of paper Jen was holding in her hand and scribbled his name on it. "Keep that someplace safe, it'll be worth a fortune someday."

"Actually," Jen smiled awkwardly, handing the paper back to Michael, "a man just asked me to give this to you."

Olivia snorted into her drink. Ellie hid a giggle behind her hand.

"Oh, yes, of course, thank you, Jen. Fans come in all shapes and sizes."

"What is it, Michael?" Ellie asked. "Did he ask for your number? Fashion advice?" she chuckled, raising a curious eyebrow.

"No," Michael said, suddenly serious. "Someone has information on George." He looked up from the handwritten note. "Jen," Michael called out, stopping her. "I'm so sorry…." He waved her back to the table. "Who gave you this note?"

"I told him I wouldn't say." Jen blushed, "I'm sorry. He gave me fifty dollars and said to make sure you get the letter." She shrugged clearly uncomfortable. "He said it was important."

"Has he ever been in here before? Is he a local?" Ellie inquired.

"I'm sorry," Jen's voice faltered. "I really can't say. He said it was important." Her eyes suddenly flew open wide, "it didn't occur to me before, he didn't... threaten you, did he?"

"No, no," Michael said reassuringly. "Everything is fine. Peculiar, but fine."

"Are you sure?" she asked hesitantly.

"Yes, I'm sure." Michael smiled harder. "You kept your word, that's a trait rarely found these days."

Jen thanked the group and walked away. Michael could tell she was battling with herself, trying to figure out if she'd done the right thing.

"You gonna clue us in," Ellie asked, "or keep us in suspense?"

He slid the paper over to Ellie and Olivia.

It read: I have information about George. Call me, followed by a phone number.

Chapter 6

Michael and Olivia piled into Ellie's Silver Acura ILX.

"Oh my God," Olivia stammered, "it's freaking freezing in here."

"Give me a second." Ellie started the car and cranked the heat up to high. "Don't worry. It warms up fast."

"Sounds like the last words someone says before they freeze to death!" Olivia exclaimed through chattering teeth.

"All right," Michael said, "I'm going to call our mysterious stranger." He jabbed the digits into his phone and selected speaker.

Moments later, a raspy voice answered.

"Hello?" Michael asked, not sure what to expect.

"Is this Michael West?"

"Yes...."

"Where are you now?"

"If the next question is 'What are you wearing?' I'm gonna insist on you buying me a drink," Michael replied.

"Last chance, Mr. West," the caller demanded.

"Fine, I'm about to leave Rumor's restaurant, but you already knew that...."

"Meet me in fifteen minutes at the Ocean Deck. Last booth on the left, beneath the swordfish. Come alone."

"Why can't you...?" Michael was speaking to a dead line.

"You aren't going to really go there and meet him, are you? It could be Drew. It could be a trap! He's been arrested for assault," Olivia reminded him.

"It's not Drew... and I don't think it's a trap."

"How do you know? He could have easily disguised his voice."

"I know because Jen knows who he is, and I trust Jen's gut."

"You're trusting someone you don't even know?"

"Even if it isn't Drew," Ellie surmised, "it could be a crazy person, maybe even someone dangerous from Drew's past."

"First, I appreciate all of the concern, but we're meeting in a very popular bar. The Ocean Deck is always crowded, so there will be plenty of people around. Second, if this was a dangerous person from his past searching for him, all he would need to do is show up at the mall. He's pretty easy to spot."

"Is there a thirdly?" Olivia asked. "Because bad news always seems to come in threes."

"Yes, it's obvious Jen knows who he is…and I'm betting we probably know who he is as well. He just wants to meet in a place a little less conspicuous. There is bad news, though," Michael continued. "I have to make it all the way down the strip in eleven minutes, in rush-hour traffic."

"But we don't…," Olivia turned toward the highway as a single car passed by "…have traffic."

"It was another attempt at humor," Ellie explained.

"I'll switch on FaceTime," Michael said as he climbed out the backseat. "That way you can listen in."

"Good idea." Ellie nodded. "And, Michael, don't do anything stupid."

"It's the Ocean Deck." Michael shrugged. "What could possibly go wrong?"

Ellie and Olivia followed Michael's red Miata down A1A, past rows of condos and hotels—all fighting over prized real estate facing the ocean.

Ellie was born in Lana Cove. She hated the thought of beautiful beachfront land being bought up by developers. As oceanfront parcels became available, the citizens of Lana Cove fought back against greedy investors by purchasing land, so they couldn't build.

"Ellie... Ellie," Olivia was talking.

Michael's right turn signal flashed red.

"Sorry." Ellie smiled, deep in thought for a moment.

"Let's park at the iHop. That way we're right across the street from the Ocean Deck if Michael needs us."

"Sounds good." Ellie braked and waited for a car to pass, then pulled into the lot. She'd just parked when her phone rang. She pressed 'accept.' Michael's smiling face appeared on her screen. "Hey, handsome."

"Hey, Ellie, I'm going to put my phone in my front pocket. Hopefully you'll be able to hear me okay."

"All right," Ellie said. "Good luck and be smart."

"Guys, I'll be fine. You're dealing with a trained professional. See you in a bit."

"Michael! Michael!"

Ellie's phone rang again.

"Sorry, I hung up," he said.

"No kidding." Ellie looked over at Olivia, who was making the sign of the cross over her chest.

🎄🎄🎄🎄

Michael stepped into the doorway of the Ocean Deck and paused, allowing for his senses to catch up to the garish interior. The smell of fried and battered food filled the air, congealing with Bob Seger belting out that he *still loves that old-time rock and roll.*

Michael tilted his head, checking out the long row of picnic tables covered in red-and-white checkered tablecloths. Greasy menus lay against the wall, between ketchup and mustard squeeze bottles. In the center of each table stood a large container of hand wipes. A card on the table let customers know they could request bibs if they ordered crabs or lobster.

A smattering of patrons sat at the bar watching Sports Center. Michael navigated to the rear of the restaurant, where a man in a black jacket and black stocking cap sat with his back to him, beneath a giant swordfish named Lucky Eddie.

The mysterious man motioned for Michael to sit across from him—he kept his head down, staring at his beer. One of Michael's exercises as a writer was to break down the components of a character: their demeanor, their clothing, and their idiosyncrasies. The old saying, actions speak louder than words, usually turned out to be true.

Whoever this man was, he didn't want to meet Michael's eyes. He hid his identity behind a stocking cap pulled low over his eyebrows. Thick black glasses perched on his nose, and he had a mustache that Michael was pretty sure was fake. His hands were tan, even in the middle of winter, which told Michael that he must spend a lot of time outside, perhaps fishing or boating.

"Put your phone on the table." The man gestured to the tabletop. He had a raspy voice, that itchy sound you usually only heard from lifelong smokers or people who drank too much dairy.

"What?" Michael wasn't sure he'd heard the man right.

"You heard me, put your phone on the table. I want to make sure no one else is listening in."

Michael gave the man an appalled expression and then slowly fished his phone out of his pocket, making sure to press the 'end call' button. Just to annoy the man, he placed it face down on the table. The man grabbed it and flipped it over.

A woman in jeans, a black t-shirt and a Santa hat appeared at the table, her arms and neck covered in tattoos. The man dipped his head, and she placed a beer in front of Michael and walked off.

"Thank you," Michael said eyeing the beer. "So, I obviously received your message. You said that you had information for me?"

"I do. I'm only talking to you because I think you have George's best interest at heart."

"You're right, I do," Michael said. "He's a good friend, and I think what happened to him is horrific."

"I do, too, and I'm risking a lot just talking to you. Understood?"

"Understood," Michael said solemnly.

"Do you know Ed Reed?"

"I know of him. I know he fired George without any explanation. But I don't know him personally."

"Mr. Reed has a lot of influence locally. His brother is the head of the town council. Most people don't know it, but he pulls the strings for many local businesses—and he has a lot of connections."

"Okay." Michael cleared his throat. "I get it. Powerful and influential, thumbs in a lot of people's pies."

"Exactly." The man pulled out his cell, swiped at the screen with his finger, and then slid it across the table to Michael.

Michael stared at the man's phone, and his heartbeat quickened. "May I?"

The man nodded.

Michael stared at the first image and then zoomed in. "She looks very familiar... I don't know who the man is though."

"The man is Ed Reed—"

"Got it. Oh, and she's the elf, and I'm guessing Drew's girlfriend."

"Swipe once more," the man replied.

Michael swiped forward. He immediately recognized Drew's car. A figure was crouched in the backseat with a camera, taking pictures. Although the figure in the image was blanketed in shadow, Michael could tell it was Drew. "How did you get these? Where were these taken?"

"At Luna's," the man said dryly. "Keep swiping, there's a few more."

"No," Michael gasped, "not the Honey Dew Motel." It was a cheap, by-the-night motel, with a less-than-reputable reputation. Picture after picture documented Ed Reed's indiscretion. There he was getting out of the car with the woman, then at the door of the motel, and then stepping into the room.

"Here's what's interesting." The man gestured to the phone. "See this next picture? That was taken two minutes after they went into the room—"

"Doesn't say much for Mr. Reed." Michael chortled, then immediately regretted it, seeing the expression on the other man's face. "Sorry… I'm a writer, vivid imagination," he said, tapping the side of his head.

"The point is, she dashed out of that room after two minutes. My guess is he made himself comfortable. She probably snapped a picture or two and then ran out."

"Wow." Michael exhaled and shook his head. "The perfect setup for blackmail, and Drew documented the whole thing." The man simply nodded. "Well, it's pretty obvious now how he got the Santa gig and the Bernstein job." Michael slid the phone back across the table. "Luna's is a pretty prestigious members-only bar, you have to be invited by a member. How did Drew's girlfriend get in?"

"Don't be naïve, Michael. She's a young, beautiful woman. For someone like that, management tends to look the other way, for *obvious* reasons."

"I see," Michael acknowledged, "but still…, Mr. Reed is well-known. I'm sure that he's *very* cautious."

"You're right, but the woman was just as cautious, and very subtle. You see, Mr. West, just like you, I am a student of human behavior, and I've developed a rather, shall we say, keen eye of picking up things that are out of place." Michael took a sip of his beer and leaned forward. He loved a good story.

"I was sitting at the far end of the bar enjoying a cocktail and a fine Cuban cigar when she came in. I noticed her because she hovered in the doorway for a moment. At first, I thought she was looking for a friend, but then she made her way to the bar and sat next to Ed."

"Was Ed alone?" asked Michael.

"He was, his friend had just left, and he was finishing up his drink when she began talking to him. She was good, she played the part of being disinterested perfectly. Even James, the bartender, didn't give the two a second glance. I was about to lose interest as well when she pulled her phone out of her purse."

"Not so unusual," said Michael.

"Not at all. I assumed she was texting someone—until she laid her phone on the bar so he could read the screen."

"She was asking him to follow her, I'm guessing," Michael said.

The man took a sip of his beer and nodded. "Exactly. He read whatever she wrote, told James he had a million things to do, paid his tab and left. She ordered another drink, sipped it for fifteen minutes or so, thanked James, and then paid her tab with cash and walked out."

"I wonder what she wrote. I mean, think about it. Ed Reed left the bar and waited outside for fifteen minutes. That's fifteen minutes of contemplating whether you're making the right decision." Michael leaned back in his seat and shook his head, "Pretty reckless if you ask me."

"I agree, especially in such a small town where everyone knows everybody else's business."

"Is Ed married?"

"Yes."

"Happily?"

"I thought so. Ed and Carol have been married thirty-five years and were inseparable. High school sweethearts, same college—I like Ed, but I think he got himself caught up in something he can't handle. George, too."

"So, she blackmails Ed. He fires George and gives Drew the job at the mall. Which by the way, still doesn't make a lot of sense to me."

"Sure it does. Drew is controlling Ed, he's making money, and he appears to be the victim in this scenario. He's just a young man trying to make a living, when he's attacked by a crazy man."

"I bet Ed helped grease the wheels for Drew to get the Santa gig at Mr. Bernstein's estate."

"I know he may seem like a dumb kid, but Drew is cleverly moving our friends around like pieces on a board game, only we don't know what game he's playing and what he gets in the end if he wins."

"I agree, but I'm not sure why you're showing me all of this. It's not going to help George get his job back, and the local news eviscerated the poor guy."

"You're a smart guy, Mr. West. I've watched you. You're furiously loyal to your friends and you're tenacious."

"How come I feel like you're about to say, 'If you choose to accept this mission—'"

"Michael, I'm just asking for a little help. I want you to go find out what Drew and this woman are up to and expose them—without wrecking Ed's life and restoring George's good name."

"Oh, that's all. Well, if you had started the conversation off with that…."

The door swung open, a young man and woman, wrapped up in coats and scarves made their way to the bar. "Look, Drew's real last name is Calvetti. He's got a record a mile long: theft, assault, bank fraud, you name it."

"All the more reason to stop him. I want you to find out what he's up to and then," the man smiled an uncomfortable smile, "we'll figure out how to get rid of him."

"I see," Michael nodded. "The problem is, he's in possession of some pretty scandalous photos. Should he feel threatened, a lot of people's lives could be ruined. And who knows, Ed may not be his only victim."

"I know, so you'll have to use discretion."

"I don't think that—"

"Look, you are already involved."

"What's that supposed to mean?"

The man sighed and flicked his finger across his phone's screen. Michael gulped—it was a picture of him breaking into Drew's car.

"How did you get that?" The man slipped his phone into his jacket and removed a thick envelope. He slid it over to Michael.

"What's this?" Michael tapped it with a finger.

"An early Christmas present," said the man, putting on his gloves. "Let's just call it an advance for your first book."

Michael pushed the envelope back to the man. "I can't take this."

"Oh, but you will, or that photo of you and several others will mysteriously arrive at Lana Cove Police Department. I need you to clear George's name. This isn't just about his livelihood, it's about his reputation. We don't know what else Drew has done—we don't need Lana Cove's community to begin toppling like dominoes."

Without another word, the man shoved the envelope back to Michael, threw a twenty on the table, stood, and walked away.

Michael sat stunned as the man exited the bar. He opened the envelope and fanned through a thick wad of hundred-dollar bills. What the heck had just happened?

His phone buzzed. He flipped it over. A text from the mysterious man's phone—he'd sent him the pictures of Ed Reed with the woman.

Michael glanced around. No one seemed to be paying any attention to him. He touched Ellie's name and sent her a quick text: *On my way, I'm okay.*

Chapter 7

"I'm telling you—it was like something out of *The Twilight Zone*," Michael said, carrying three piping-hot cups of Earl Grey tea into the living room. "Be right back." He hurried into the kitchen and came back moments later with sugar, honey, and spoons.

"Can I give you a hand?" Olivia asked, watching Michael disappear into the kitchen for the third time.

"No, it's my last trip," he shouted. He returned with a plate stacked with pastries. "Harry and David cookies," Michael explained. "They're from my old boss in Boston. He's still trying to lure me back, one delicious treat at a time."

"Is it working?" asked Olivia.

"I am motivated by calories," Michael divulged.

"That's nice." Ellie grabbed a coconut macaroon. "But he'll just have to accept the fact that you're ours now, so hands off."

"Agreed." Olivia laughed. "But let him down slowly so he keeps sending cookies."

"So, you said that you had hush-hush information. What did you find out?" Ellie asked.

"Ladies, you're not going to believe this one. Our mystery man had photos of Ed Reed with the elf," Michael said.

"What kind of photos?" Ellie asked, knowing there was more to the story.

"These." Michael opened the images on his phone. "Swipe through them, they kind of speak for themselves."

Olivia took the phone, a look of apprehension on her face. "Is that Drew with a camera in another car?"

"Yep, Drew captured the whole thing. He's blackmailing Ed. That's how he got the Santa gig."

"Oh my, they went to the Honey Dew Motel," gasped Olivia.

"Ed's toast!" exclaimed Ellie. "As long as Drew has these, he controls him."

"So what do we do? Go to the police?" Olivia asked. "Say that we have proof that an ex-con is extorting Ed Reed?"

"We can't," said Ellie. "If we expose Drew, who's to stop him or his assistant from sending those pictures to the news, or Ed's wife."

"Yep, this whole thing could unravel like an ugly Christmas sweater."

"Plus we'd have a homicide on her hands, his wife would kill him," stated Ellie. "I've seen her on the golf course, she'd club him to death."

"And don't forget the church—he's the head deacon. Ed has a lot to lose."

"And like I told the mystery man, we don't know who else they've done this to. So far, we only know about Ed."

"Honestly, at this point, Ed may want to take the option of telling his wife that he was fooled by a professional con artist," Olivia surmised.

"It would be the noble, right thing to do," Michael acknowledged, "but I don't see that happening. Plus, we don't know if he has anything else that he's holding over Ed's head."

"So we do nothing?" Ellie asked, exasperated. "And meanwhile, George looks like the town idiot, and this crazy convict is calling all the shots?"

"It's not like we're *not* doing anything," Michael insisted, "we're finding out everything we can about Drew, and we're trying to see if we can pin this other crime on him. And," he added, "I don't know Ed personally, but I'm sure he'll come to some sort of arrangement with Drew. He's not going to be under his thumb forever."

The trio jumped as a loud *knock, knock, knock* came from the back door.

Ellie and Olivia looked at Michael. He shrugged and jumped to his feet—he was just as confused as they were about this late-night visitor.

He hurried through the kitchen, followed by Ellie and Olivia, and flicked on the back light. George stood on his porch, dressed in his Santa suit, peering around anxiously.

"George," Michael blurted, throwing open the door. "Come in." He stepped aside as George rushed into the house, his face pale as if he'd seen a ghost, his eyes wild—he smelled of cigarettes and old coffee.

"George, are you okay?" Ellie grabbed his hand. "You're freezing."

George turned to Ellie, his voice a hoarse whisper, "He's dead, Ellie, he's dead."

"Who's dead? George!"

"Drew's dead, and the police think I killed him."

"Why on earth would they possibly think that?"

"Turn on the news," he said with an abrupt wave of his hand. "It's all over the news."

Michael hurried into the living room. "Where's the remote?" he shouted.

"On the coffee table," Ellie said, joining him and Olivia in the living room.

Michael grabbed the remote and flicked through the channels to the local news. Olivia helped George onto the sofa.

A newswoman stood on the side of the street beneath a spotlight, wrapped in a brown winter coat, stocking cap, and Burberry scarf. Snow swirled around her, coating her hat and coat in glistening powdery flakes. She pointed to a house surrounded by police officers and emergency workers. Television vans and police cars lined the street in front of a large Victorian-styled home.

"George," Ellie turned to him, "that's your house!"

George nodded and closed his eyes—it was a nightmare that would never end.

A cluster of CSU officers busily secured the crime scene. Yellow police tape stretched around the entirety of the property. The news cameraman zoomed in, showing a miniature sleigh being pulled by eight tiny reindeer. The sleigh was crushed, and on top of the sleigh, Drew's body.

"Oh my God." Ellie's hand flew to her mouth.

The camera moved from George's yard, back to the newswoman. "This is the scene in front of the home of George Owens—longtime Lana Cove native—where the body of Drew Small was found."

George's picture appeared on the screen—the news station decided to use a picture from when the security guards had escorted him out of the mall.

"According to Officer Reynolds, Drew Small was shot in the chest and then *thrown* from the second-story balcony…" The reporter turned and gestured toward a snow-covered balcony, a conspicuous section, where Drew had been launched over the railing was free of snow. The cameraman followed her commentary with his camera. "…and he crashed onto the sleigh below."

The cameraman mimicked the fall by zooming in on the balcony and quickly lowering the camera to the sled. The camera then panned back to the news reporter. She nodded solemnly before beginning again.

"So far, the police are keeping tight-lipped about the details. However, an anonymous caller said that he saw Mr. Small in a heated argument with Mr. Owens at the Schooners restaurant shortly before his death. We are still waiting for Mr. Owens's arrival. Police are asking—for anyone with information regarding this crime or Mr. Owens's whereabouts—to please call the Lana Cove Police Department."

The telephone number for the Lana Cove Police Department scrolled across the bottom of the screen.

"George," Ellie pleaded, "what's going on? We know you didn't do this."

"No, no, for God's sake, Ellie, of course not. I had just finished up at the Bernstein party."

"Wait, the Bernstein party?" questioned Michael. "I thought that you—"

"I'll explain everything," said George, waving away Michael's outburst. "I was on my way home and I stopped to get gas and coffee at Waverly's. As I'm getting my coffee, I hear the name of my street on the news. I look up and see my house, surrounded by the police on the television. And then... I see Drew sprawled on top of my sled. I didn't know where to go, so I came here. I know it probably wasn't the best decision, but I panicked. I'm so sorry to put you guys in the middle of this—"

"It's okay, it's okay," Ellie assured him. "We'll figure this out."

"It's just that, with the whole thing at the mall... and then, someone kills Drew in my front yard."

George shook his head. "It's too much for an old man, Ellie."

"George, let me see your hand—it's bleeding," Michael said gently.

"It's nothing," George said a little too quickly. "I just slipped on some ice out back. Really, it's nothing."

"Olivia, there's a first-aid kit in the closet beside the bathroom, do you mind?"

"Not at all," Olivia hurried off down the hallway.

"George, start from the beginning," Ellie suggested, taking a seat beside him on the sofa. "Tell us everything that happened over the past few hours. Every little detail."

"Okay." George licked his chapped lips and rubbed his nose. "I was just sitting down to eat dinner when my phone rang. The number showed up as unknown, so I didn't answer it, but then they called again. I was about to give whoever it was an earful about calling at dinnertime, when the guy tells me that it's Drew and that he needed to talk to me in person."

"Drew called you?" Ellie was shocked.

"Yes, I couldn't believe it either," said George, seeing Ellie's expression. "He told me to bring my suit and meet him at Schooners right away if I wanted my job back. I got so excited, I figured maybe he had talked to Ed, and he'd had a change of heart."

"I imagine you dropped everything and went to Schooners to meet him," Michael surmised.

"You bet your life I did. I could tell as soon as I saw him though, that something wasn't right. He was panicky—he kept watching the door, looking all around."

"Any idea why?" Michael asked.

"Not at the time. Like I said, I knew something had him spooked. He hurries over to me and tells me that I can have all my Santa jobs back on one condition. He pulled out this black book and said that he needed me to give it to someone at the Bernstein's party."

"What did you say?" Ellie asked.

"That part was easy—I told him no way. I mean, I had no idea what was in that book, or where it came from. Something about the whole situation didn't seem right."

"I'll say," muttered Michael.

"He obviously wasn't expecting me to say no because he threw me against the wall and told me I had to take the book. The look he had in his eyes, Ellie... I was scared to death—I thought he was going to kill me. I tried to leave, but he shoved me against the wall again. I tripped and fell, and he ran out the door."

"George, you could have been badly hurt. No one tried to help you?"

"A couple of kids—well, I call them kids—came over after Drew left—it all happened so fast. I felt like I was in a daze. I told them that it was just a misunderstanding and hurried outside." Ellie gave him a look and shook her head. "I know," George acknowledged her disapproval. "Not my finest hour."

"So, Drew ran off with the book? Did he get in a car? Was he being followed?" asked Ellie.

"Yes, I saw him running toward his car. The elf girl from the mall was sitting inside with the motor running, revving the engine. He must have stepped on some ice or something because he slipped and landed hard, smacking his head. All of a sudden, these two guys start chasing him."

"Did you get a look at the two men?" asked Michael.

"No, I just remember blue jeans, dark winter jackets and black knit hats. They almost got Drew though. They were hanging onto his door as Drew and his girlfriend sped away."

"What did the two men do after that?" Ellie prompted George.

"They climbed in a black Mustang and tore out of the parking lot after them."

"I guess it's too much to hope for that you got a license plate number?"

"I'm sorry, Michael. The only thing that was on my mind was to get out of there. If they were coming back, I didn't want to be around."

"That's smart," Ellie agreed. "Is that when you left Schooners?"

"Yes, I went home, showered, and then went to the Bernsteins. Seems like Drew was so sure that I was going to accept the book, he had Ed call them for me."

"That's wonderful," said Ellie. "Well, at least, that part of the story—"

"Oh," said George, reaching into his pocket. "I found this… Drew must have dropped it when he fell and hit his head."

"Drew dropped it?" Michael asked.

George nodded. "I'm pretty sure. I found it right where he fell."

"One sec," Michael said excitedly, "I'll get my laptop."

Olivia and Ellie cleared the coffee table as Michael disappeared upstairs. Moments later, he returned and placed his laptop on the table.

"Okay, let's see what we got," Michael said, pushing the memory card into the side of the computer.

Ellie, Olivia, and George huddled in a semicircle around him.

A folder appeared on the screen, simply named DCIM.

"What's DCIM?" George asked. "Some kind of code?"

"Nothing nefarious." Michael clicked on the folder. "It stands for Digital Camera Images." The folder opened, revealing rows of pictures and video files. Michael clicked the *View* menu option and selected *Extra Large Icons*. The pictures instantly tripled in size.

"That's Ed, and… that's not his wife," George declared, his eyes growing wide. "That's the elf woman."

"It's the reason you were fired," Michael explained. "Drew was blackmailing Ed Reed." The folder contained additional photos of Ed in various stages of undress on the motel bed.

"Oh my Lord!" George gasped. "This is going to destroy his wife… his daughter. It's going to end his career."

"Michael, these aren't just pictures of Edward," Ellie said. "Look, these are photos from the November Art Expo. I helped cater the event."

"And there's Mrs. Mallory," Olivia said, pointing at the screen. "She just had a seventy-thousand-dollar necklace stolen," she explained to George. "We think Drew is somehow connected, we're just not sure how yet."

Michael clicked forward to the next image.

"There's a close-up." Ellie jabbed her finger at the screen. "Not that I've seen a lot of seventy-thousand-dollar necklaces, but that certainly looks like one."

"It's stunning," Olivia said.

"So, she still had the necklace when this photo was taken…. Wasn't the expo at the beginning of November?" Michael asked.

"It was November seventeenth, my mom's birthday," Olivia said.

"So, Drew was in town then… according to his motel parking pass."

"And you think Drew stole it?" George asked.

"We do," Ellie replied. "These photos are pretty damning. See how he zoomed in on the necklace in this photo?"

"I have to admit, he did his research. People love to dress up and show off their wealth at the art expo. It's a virtual who's who of the social elite of Lana Cove," George acknowledged.

"There's another example." Olivia gestured to a picture of a woman in a cocktail dress and a stunning diamond tennis bracelet. "That bracelet must be worth at least ten thousand dollars."

"At least," Ellie said, clearly stunned by the vast collection of images. "He's got dozens of pictures of jewelry."

"Not only jewelry." Michael nodded. "But people's houses."

"That's Mrs. Mallory's home," Ellie interrupted, "and that's Robert Neilson's house, there's the Bernstein estate, the Bono house…."

"Who in the world is that?" Olivia asked.

The last two rows of photos showed a man dressed in khakis and a gray button-down shirt. He didn't look the part of a mover or a shaker, Drew's usual target. The man in the photo was gawking at the elf woman. In the next picture, he was handing her a beer and then helping her with her coat.

"I'm not sure." Ellie turned to her friends.

They all shook their heads.

"Check out the background," Olivia said.

Ellie and Michael leaned in closer. Two women sat at the bar, facing toward the man, staring angrily. One of the women was holding a phone in her hand, obviously taking pictures. "Someone's not happy," Olivia observed.

"Our mystery man has a wedding ring, too…," Ellie pointed out.

"If those women are doing what I think they're doing, that man's belongings are going to be in his front yard when he gets home," Michael said. "Hell hath no fury like a woman scorned."

"How does he even fit into the picture?" Olivia asked. "He certainly doesn't appear to be rich."

"Not sure," Michael replied. "Have you ever seen him before, George?" He zoomed in on the man's face.

"Sorry." George shook his head. "He doesn't look familiar."

"Michael, zoom in on his chair. If that's his jacket…" Ellie gestured to a gray jacket draped over a chair behind the man, "…it has a logo on it. It may give us some idea as to who he is."

"You are brilliant!" Michael exclaimed. He clicked on the magnifying glass icon, and using the mouse, moved the image so the jacket was in the center of the screen. A burgundy patch with gray letters that spelled P.E.W. was attached to the sleeve.

Michael opened Google and typed the words *Lana Cove P.E.W.* into the search box. Seconds later, the return results revealed *Precision Electrical Works*. He clicked on the link. An aged website that appeared as though it had been designed as an after-school project loaded.

"Wow," Olivia frowned, "that's a *lot* of gray and red...."

Michael quickly skimmed the contents of the page. "They're a local company." He read a bit more. "They specialize in home and small business electrical installation and repair... and bingo, it seems our mystery man is none other than Tony Meyer, owner and electrical operations specialist."

"Let's hope his website isn't a representation of his skill level," said Ellie.

Olivia agreed, nodding. "So the question is, why would Drew and his girlfriend get involved with an electrical contractor?"

"No idea... the man's obviously married, and from what we can see in the picture, he's once again using the blackmail element."

"Geesh," Olivia frowned, "men simply cannot be trusted." Her face reddened and she turned to George, "Except for you," she grabbed his arm gently, "you're perfect."

"What if," Ellie exclaimed excitedly, "Drew needed an electrician's expertise for one of his jobs?! Perhaps cut the power to an alarm system? I don't know—I'm just hypothesizing here."

"That actually makes sense. They get pictures of this guy," Michael said, "and they threaten to show his wife. All he has to do is help disable a couple of alarms...."

"And they'll *promise* to destroy the pictures once they get what they want," Ellie said.

"Drew was casting a dangerous net," Michael said. "This town isn't very big. I mean, there's no way he could have sustained this type of behavior in such a small community. It's like playing Russian roulette. Eventually—"

"Eventually, you're going to wind up dead," Olivia said matter-of-factly.

"That's right," Ellie agreed. "He probably thought that if he had enough dirt on influential people, that no one could touch him."

"Or push him," Michael smirked.

"So, who do you think killed him?" Olivia asked.

"If I had to guess," Michael said, "it would be the person who had the most to lose."

"You think it was Ed, don't you?"

Michael gave George a look that said he wasn't going to deny it.

"Here's the deal. I know Ed's a scoundrel and a jerk," George bellowed, "but I've known him and his family for nearly twenty years. This isn't something he's capable of doing."

"I hope not," Ellie reassured him, "but having Drew out of the way would certainly make his life a *lot* easier. He—"

"He didn't do it," George cut her off, crossing his arms over his chest defiantly. "I mean, for all you know, it could have been me."

"George!" Ellie glared at him sternly. "Why would you say that?"

"Ed's a lot of things, but he's *not* a murderer."

"Well," Ellie sighed, "at least you have an airtight alibi. You were at the Bernstein's house when all of this happened, and you've got dozens of witnesses."

"Was Ed at the party, George?" Olivia asked.

"I don't know, I can't remember. There were so many people there… and I was still pretty rattled from the incident at the Schooners. I'm sure he was."

"I hate to say it," Michael said, "but right now, George is most likely the prime suspect."

"Michael!" Ellie snapped, "What are you doing?"

"Ellie," Michael held up his hands, "please let me explain. Right now, the police have no idea about Ed being blackmailed, they have no idea about Tony being blackmailed—the last person who witnesses saw with Drew alive was George. This memory card shows that multiple people had motive to kill Drew. George, we're going to have to turn this over to the police."

"I know…," George replied quietly.

"Do you have a good lawyer?" Michael asked. "The police are going to want to question you."

George's face turned pale.

Ellie reached out and took his hand. It felt cold and frail. "You're going to be fine." She smiled gently. "You have a strong alibi, and the memory card is going to show the police what Drew was up to."

George nodded. "You're right, Ellie, I just don't want anything to happen to Ed or his family. I'll give Gordon Sparks a call—he'll know what to do."

"You can use my guest room if you would like some privacy," Michael offered.

"Thank you." George squeezed Ellie's hand, retraced his steps down the hallway to the guest room, and shut the door.

"Look," Michael said when they were alone, "I know that George thinks Ed is innocent, but honestly, I think he's the prime suspect. We know it's not George, and it couldn't be Mrs. Mallory—

she could barely lift a five-pound bag of sugar—and her husband, well, he wears pleated pants and Izod Lacoste sweaters, so enough said."

"It could be Tony, the electrical worker," Olivia suggested.

"Maybe," Ellie said, "but from what we saw, he was acting like a total imbecile, but it didn't escalate to the same level as Ed… well," she corrected herself, "at least we don't have evidence that he went as far as Ed."

"We're forgetting a huge piece of the puzzle," said Olivia. "The black book."

"That's right." Ellie nodded. "He tried to get George to deliver the book to someone at the party."

"Which meant Drew couldn't do it himself… he already knew he was in trouble," Michael suggested.

"I wonder if he stole the book, realized what was inside, and then decided he was in way over his head," Ellie suggested.

"I think you're right," Michael said. "However, the only person that's going to know the answer—"

"Is his accomplice," Ellie said, completing Michael's thought.

"We've got to get to the Beach Comber Motel," Olivia stated, "before she skips town."

The trio pulled on their winter coats as they waited for George to finish his phone call. Ellie pressed the button on her fob to warm up her car.

"Are you guys heading out?" George inquired, surprised that everyone had their coats on.

"Yes," Michael replied, "we've got a lead that we want to chase down. Were you able to get in touch with Gordon?"

"Yes, yes, he's going to pick me up here. I mean," George smiled, somewhat embarrassed, "if it's okay that I stay here."

"Certainly, that's fine with me, make yourself at home." Michael paused in the doorway. "George, are you sure Drew didn't say anything about who you were supposed to give the book to?"

George hesitated, his gaze dropping to the floor. "No, Michael, I'm sorry. Just that it was someone at the Bernstein party."

Michael couldn't help but feel George was hiding something from them. He decided to push just a little more. "Yeah, almost impossible to figure out *who*. There was probably over a hundred people there."

"At least," George said.

"Did you see anything inside the book, or maybe initials on the cover, anything?"

"Nothing," George replied. "It was a black book with a leather cover, the size of an address book."

"We need to go, Michael," Ellie insisted. "We're running out of time."

Chapter 8

The Beach Comber Motel was located on the outskirts of Lana Cove cocooned between a nearly empty strip mall and a mobile home lot. The motel had recently been painted a latte brown with white trim, making it look like the world's saddest gingerbread house. The rooms were tiny, rectangular boxes aligned in a row, each door decorated with a flimsy, plastic Christmas wreath with a red plastic bow.

A neon-yellow oval sign sat balanced atop a blue-neon ocean wave. The oval sign was split into halves: the bottom was sandy brown and decorated with seashells, the top a brilliant blue. The words *Beach Comber Motel* beckoned to the discreet, and the bright neon-red vacancy let passersby know they were available to entertain their transgressions for only twenty-nine dollars a night.

Ellie eased her car into the motel lot and pulled in between a Jeep and a pickup truck, the back filled with snow-covered firewood.

Three police cars, lights flashing, were parked in front of the motel. The door to room number seventeen was open, and a uniformed officer watched them warily as they exited Ellie's car.

"That's not a good sign," Ellie said under her breath.

"Olivia, Ellie," Michael whispered, grabbing Ellie by the sleeve of her jacket. "That blue Honda." He tilted his head. "That's Drew's car."

"Oh no." Ellie shook her head, worried about the safety of the elf woman. "I should have called the police—"

Suddenly, a man burst out the door of room seventeen, his hands cuffed behind his back, followed by two police officers.

"I already told you! I heard yelling, the door was open, I just wanted to make sure she was okay! How was I supposed to know it was the television? I'm a hero."

"That's the guy from the pictures," Olivia said. "Tony, the electrician."

"Livs, there's Ryan." Ellie pointed at one of the officers escorting Tony to the back of the squad car.

"Ask my wife, she'll tell you!" Tony shouted. "I was only trying to straighten things out." He nodded toward a red-haired woman, bundled in a blue winter coat, an angry expression on her face.

"Yeesh, that guy might be safer in jail," Michael joked quietly.

"I think you're right," Olivia said. "That's one angry woman."

"Ryan," Ellie called out, waving to him.

The officer looked up, stared for a moment, and then his face relaxed when he recognized her. He spoke to his partner—Ellie imagined he was telling him that he knew her—and then he walked over. "Ellie, what are you doing here?"

"Helping Mr. West here do a little sleuthing," Ellie said, arching an eyebrow. "Ryan, this is Michael West, future bestselling author, but mostly just unemployed."

Ryan gave Michael the once-over and then reached out and shook his hand.

"And you know Livs," Ellie said.

"Yes, of course. Hi, Olivia." Ryan gave her an awkward smile and an even more awkward wave, which Michael could tell he immediately regretted.

"Is she okay? The woman, is she okay?" Ellie asked before Ryan could ask her any more questions.

"Luckily, she wasn't here, but we did find this guy going through her stuff. Claims she—"

"Detective Mitchell," the other police officer called out, motioning him over.

"Just a minute," Ryan said, rolling his eyes. "Let me go see what Baxter needs. I'll be right back."

"One quick question," Ellie said. "Why is he after the woman who was staying here?"

"Long story short, he claims that he came here to confront her. Said she came on to him at a bar. Said they shared a couple drinks, the woman gave him a hug and left. Unfortunately for him, a couple of his wife's friends were at the bar and snapped some pictures of him with the woman. He said he brought his wife here to prove nothing happened."

"And he heard screaming inside," Ellie added, "so he burst into the room to make sure she was okay?"

"Yeah." Ryan nodded. "The television was really loud—I'll give him that. We got an anonymous tip that an assault was in progress, so we hightailed it over here and found this gentleman in her room. I'm sorry, I gotta see what Officer Jackson needs."

"Sure, sure, thank you, Ryan."

"So," Olivia asked as Ryan walked away, "do you think Tony's telling the truth?"

"My gut tells me yes," Ellie replied, "and I think Ryan's does, too. Who would bring their wife over here to confront another woman if he was going to do something… insane? I'm going to talk to his wife. You two wait here, I think she'll be more receptive if it's just one person and not three."

"Fair enough. Come on, Michael." Olivia motioned toward Ellie's car. "I think we've just been relegated to the children's table."

"Fine." Michael sniffed defiantly, a devious twinkle in his eyes. "Don't be surprised if we have this entire case solved by time you get back."

"I won't hold my breath." Ellie disappeared inside the motel's office and returned a minute later with a hot cup of coffee. "Heck of a night," she said to the woman, who'd just watched her husband being led off in handcuffs. "Here's a cup of coffee."

"Thank you."

Ellie guessed the woman was about forty, her eyes tired, her cheeks and nose red from the cold. She cradled the cup for a moment, blew across the rim, and took a sip.

"Horrible night." She shook her head. "And who are you? Are you with the police department? You seem familiar."

"No, ma'am, I'm Ellie Banks. I own the Bitter Sweet Café."

"That's right." The woman smiled wanly. "I've been there several times. Delicious coffee, and a lovely atmosphere. My name's Rita. So—"

"Yes," Ellie explained, "you're wondering why I'm, well, we," she gestured to Michael and Olivia, "are here."

The woman tilted her head and raised her eyebrows, as if to say: Well, don't just stand there, tell me.

"We were driving down Ridgewood, and we saw the police cars. I recognized my friend over there," she pointed at Officer Ryan, "he's the guy talking on his phone, and, well, my curiosity got the better of me, so I stopped to see what was going on."

"Yeah, seems like curiosity got ahold of my husband, too—he's the idiot over there in handcuffs." She glanced at him and shook her head. "I've been married to him for twenty years— this Tuesday is our twenty-first anniversary—and this is what I get: My husband gawking at some spring chicken. And then to make matters worse, he gets arrested breaking into her motel room."

"I'm so sorry… but why would he be barging into a woman's motel room? And why would he bring you? That doesn't make sense."

"It's nothing," the woman said bitterly. She sipped her drink and waved as if shooing away the conversation.

Ellie took a gulp of her coffee and stared out at the parking lot, giving the woman her space.

"Ah, what the heck…. Tony's a good guy," she started. "He's smart, but he doesn't have any common sense. He admitted to buying the young harlot a couple of beers and giving her a hug, but he said that was as far as it went, and I believe him."

"Men's egos are so fragile. He made a mistake. I can understand why you would be mad."

"I'm not really mad about him buying someone a beer, I'm mad because she stole his wallet. He said she went to the restroom and never returned—he figured she'd just used him to get a couple free drinks. But, when he went to pay his tab, he realized his wallet was missing."

"Oh," Ellie grimaced, "and how did you end up here?"

"Tony put two and two together, ran out into the parking lot just in time to see her jump into a blue car with Florida plates and speed off. That's the car," she said, pointing at the blue Honda. "By the time he got to his car, she was long gone."

"How the heck did you two ever find her?"

"It took almost a day and a half. He figured she was from out of town because of the Florida plates. So, he mapped off Lana Cove, and we have been to every bed and breakfast, hotel and motel in this little town."

"And you decided to come with him?"

"After you get texts and photos from your friends that your husband is buying another woman drinks, and then your husband declares he's going to search all of Lana Cove until he finds her...." Rita's eyes filled with tears. "I love my Tony, but I don't like being made a fool of, and because of his stupidity, he'll probably lose a huge contract at the Bono estate."

"Wait, how would he lose his job? I'm sure Mr. Bono would understand that you had to take care of a few things since your husband's wallet was stolen."

"I wish it were that simple," Rita explained. "I couldn't care less about the woman. It's just that, we really needed this contract. The Bonos have a very strict security protocol for employees. Tony's been working for six weeks to get approved to work at their estate. He's been through background checks, his company has been investigated, and they even ran a background check on me. He was supposed to begin work today."

"I guess I'm just being dense," Ellie said, "but if your husband passed the background check, and they verified the legitimacy of his business…."

"The problem is what was in his wallet. My husband was given a super-encrypted, all-access key card to the Bono estate. To put it simply, you *do not* lose this card. Now they would have to reissue cards for all of their staff and recode their alarm systems. That's the reason this is all so heartbreaking. This was a high-paying job and also a tremendous opportunity for Tony to make a name for himself and to land higher-paying clientele. Now, it's all over."

Ellie put her hand on Rita's shoulder. "Maybe not. Listen, Officer Ryan is great—I've known him since high school. I'll do what I can for you and your husband, maybe they'll find that wallet, and he won't have to make that call…."

"Thank you so much. Tony's a good guy, too, he's never been in trouble."

Ellie handed Rita her phone. "Type in your number, and I'll let you know what I find out. I'll do whatever I can do, I promise you."

The woman nodded, jabbed in her number, and handed over the phone. She closed her eyes, tears streaming down her cheeks. "Thank you," she whispered quietly as Ellie walked away.

Chapter 9

"So nice of you to return, Ellie. I'll have you know that in your absence, we busted the case wide open!" Michael exclaimed.

"Really?"

Michael nodded and then shook his head. "Nope, we've got nothing. We know it's not George—"

"I can almost guarantee it's not this guy," Ellie said. "His wife's been playing *Where's Waldo* with him for the past thirty-six hours."

"I saw you speaking with Tony's wife." Officer Ryan joined the group. "Want to compare stories?"

"Sure, Rita said that her husband met the harlot—her words not mine—at a bar, that he'd bought her a couple drinks, she went in for a hug—and relieved him of his wallet. He realized his wallet was missing when he went to pay his tab, and she claims that they've spent most of the past thirty-six hours scouring Lana Cove for her car."

Ryan nodded. "Did she say anything about how he got into the room?"

"She didn't mention that. She *did* mention that he'd just landed a very important contracting job at the Bono estate, and the wallet had his new security card in there. I have a feeling that it was more about getting that card back than anything."

"The Bono compound is like a fortress," Ryan concurred. "Losing that security card definitely isn't going to bode well for Tony."

"What's going to happen to him?" Ellie stole a look at the man sitting in the squad car, his chin against his chest.

"We'll bring him and his wife in for questioning—at this point he's looking at criminal trespass—but we'll see what the captain says."

"Did you find his wallet?" Michael asked.

"We did." Ryan nodded. "The credit cards, cash, and security card were gone."

"You didn't happen to find a little black book, did you, like an address book?" Ellie asked.

Officer Ryan closed his notebook and narrowed his eyes. "Ellie Banks, what aren't you telling me?"

Ellie kicked herself. "You know George, George Owens?"

"Yes, and if you know of his whereabouts, Ellie, he is a suspect in a homicide investigation."

"George showed up at Michael's house...."

Ryan's mouth tightened into a thin line.

"Ryan, this was *before* we knew anything had happened."

"Where is George now?"

"After we found out Drew had been killed, and George was a suspect, we told him he needed to turn himself over to the police. He called Gordon Sparks, his lawyer. They were on their way to the Lana Cove police department."

Ryan sighed. Ellie could tell he was upset with her, and rightfully so.

"What did George tell you?" he asked.

"He said Drew called him and told him to meet him at the Schooners restaurant if he wanted his job back. He said he needed him to do a favor for him, that he would explain the details in person."

"We have numerous witness accounts," Ryan confirmed, "that placed George at Schooners with Drew. Did he say anything else?"

"He told George he had a black book and he needed him to give it to someone at the Bernstein party. According to George, Drew acted like it was life or death. It frightened George so much that he refused to get involved."

"Did he say to whom he was supposed to give the book to?"

"No. But George did say that Drew kept looking around nervously. He even tried to force George to take the book, but when he wouldn't, George said Drew slammed him into the wall and took off running." Ellie reached into her pocket and handed Ryan the memory card. "He said Drew dropped this when he slipped and fell on ice running to his car."

"Any idea what's on it?" Ryan asked.

"It's basically filled with photos of people Drew was blackmailing, pictures from the art expo, people's homes… a virtual who's who connecting Drew to a huge web of crimes."

"George gave you this card?"

"Yes, when he showed up at Michael's. He found it when he was walking to his car, on the ground where Drew slipped."

"Hmm." Ryan pulled out a baggie and placed the memory card inside. "Ellie, you said George told you he would get his job back if he delivered the book to someone at the Bernstein party?"

"That's right. George told me and my friends that it wasn't until he left the Bernsteins, and stopped for coffee at Waverly's, that he found out Drew had been killed. He saw the report on the news, saw Drew in his front yard, panicked, and drove straight to Michael's house."

"I just want to say," Michael spoke up, "that my house is not a safe haven for individuals wanted by the police. Please continue, Ellie."

Ryan's jaw tightened. "Ellie, George didn't work the Bernstein party. My family went to it—and the Santa they had definitely wasn't George."

"What?" Ellie gasped, she felt like she'd been punched in the gut. "But he told us…. Why would he lie to us?"

Officer Ryan fished his cell phone out of his pocket and punched in a series of numbers.

Michael, Ellie, and Olivia stood breathlessly waiting.

"Miller, it's Detective Mitchell. Has George Owens been processed?"

The sound came of fingers flying across a keyboard. "No, sir, it's a quiet night."

"Thanks, Miller. If he arrives, let me know ASAP."

"Yes, sir."

Ryan looked at the group and rubbed his head. "Seems like George is in the wind. Do me a favor, Ellie, let me know immediately if you see him—he could be dangerous."

Ellie closed her eyes—she wanted to vomit. How had everything turned out so wrong?

Chapter 10

Numb, Ellie climbed into her freezing car with Michael and Olivia. She took her phone from her pocket and dialed George's number. It went straight to voicemail.

"Ellie, we need to get back to my house. We need to find out if George is still there," Michael said.

"He lied to us… why would George lie to us?"

"He's afraid, Ellie," Michael said, touching her shoulder. "He's not thinking straight."

Ellie started the engine and pressed the front and rear defrost buttons. The tires made a crunching sound in the snow as she backed out of the parking space. On the display from her rear backup camera, she could see Rita hunched over, her head in her hands. She felt a comradery with the woman—they'd both been deceived by people they cared deeply about.

"Ellie, maybe we should try calling George's lawyer... what was his name? Gordon something," Olivia suggested.

"Gordon Sparks," Ellie replied, turning onto Ridgewood.

"I'll see if I can find his number," Michael volunteered. He pulled up Google on his phone and searched for Gordon Sparks Esquire. "Found him." He tapped the speaker button.

The phone rang several times and then went to voicemail.

"Great." Michael sighed. "I'll leave a message. Hopefully he checks his—"

"Wait," Olivia interrupted, "he's giving an afterhours emergency number."

Michael opened his notepad app and quickly typed in the telephone number. "Got it."

Olivia met Ellie's eyes in the rearview mirror. This was hard on both of them. George was a close friend, and now he'd lied to them and may have killed a man.

"Hello." Michael's voice cut through the silence. He tapped the speaker button again and turned up the volume. "I'm Michael West, I'm a good friend of George Owens. I'm sorry for the late hour, I wouldn't call if this wasn't urgent."

"Hello, Michael, what's this about?" Gordon's voice was clipped and direct.

"I'm not sure if you've seen the news this evening, but a man was killed in George's front yard, and George is the police's main suspect."

"Yes," Gordon exhaled loudly, "I did see the news. I tried calling him several times, but the calls went straight to voicemail."

Michael looked at Ellie, another lie, another punch to the gut. She veered off the road into a Wawa gas station.

"So, George hasn't tried contacting you?" Michael asked.

"No, not this evening." Concern grew in the man's voice. "Tell me *exactly* what's going on."

"George came to my house when he found out Drew… had been murdered. He told me he was worried about the police suspecting that he was to blame."

"And indeed he should. A man was murdered on his property. I don't understand why he went to your house instead of contacting the police, or me. This doesn't sound like George, he's usually very rational."

"At the moment, nothing makes sense. There was the mall incident with Drew that went viral, and then George got into a fight with him at

Schooners, and a couple hours later, Drew wound up dead in his front yard."

"Schooners? What in the world was George doing at that dive?"

"Meeting Drew. He promised to give George his job back. As soon as we found out he was in trouble, I asked George if he had a lawyer. He went into my guest bedroom to call you."

"Only he never did." Michael could hear the disappointment in Gordon's voice.

"The last conversation I had with George was that he was going to the police station with you to clear everything up. Now, no one can find him."

"You spoke with the police department?"

"Yes, with dispatch. He never turned himself in."

"Thank you for your call, Michael. If you hear anything, please call me immediately."

"Yes sir, I will. If you would also, let us know if you hear from him. Everyone is terribly worried about him. We just want to make sure he's okay."

"I will. I take it the number you are calling from is your cell number."

"Yes, sir."

"Okay, I'll be in touch if I hear anything. I'll call the police station for an update. Have a good evening."

"Good night." Michael hung up and turned toward Ellie. Dark thoughts filled his mind. He quickly said a silent prayer that George hadn't done anything to hurt himself.

Olivia leaned forward from the back between the two front seats. "This has been a horrible night."

"I need some coffee and some fresh air!" Ellie exclaimed, pushing her door open.

"I second that," Olivia said.

Michael unfastened his seatbelt and hurried around the front of the car to join the girls. He caught Ellie's shoulder as she slipped on black ice.

"Thanks," she grabbed Michael's arm, and pulled herself against him.

Olivia shook her head as they traversed the icy parking lot. "Like the blind leading the blind."

"Oh hush, get in here, you," said Ellie, interlocking her other arm with Olivia.

"Listen, I have a theory. So far just about everything George has told us over the past twelve hours has been a lie."

Ellie gave him a pained look. She bit her lip, holding back tears.

"I'm sorry, Ellie, but it's true. Bernstein's party, calling his lawyer—"

"Okay, okay, so what's your point? I refuse to believe that George killed someone. I've known him my entire life. People don't just change."

"He snapped at the mall," Michael said. "Remember the entire beard incident? The truth is, we never know what will set someone off."

A bell tinkled as Ellie pushed open the door to the service station. She blinked at the harsh fluorescent overhead lights washing over them. Michael and Olivia followed at her heels as she made a beeline to the back of the store, to the coffee counter.

"Hazelnut's fresh," a short, balding guy in a burgundy vest yelled out. He pointed at various pots of coffee. "French vanilla is fresh, and the pecan blend. The rest was made about three hours ago."

"Thank you," Olivia shouted back.

"Listen," Michael continued gently, pouring himself a large cup of hazelnut. "Remember when George said Drew kept trying to force the book on him, and he wouldn't take it? What if he did? Remember how he acted when I asked him about it?"

"I don't know, it's a reach," said Ellie.

"Look, one thing we know about George is he has a huge heart. Maybe, just maybe, he lied to us about the black book, and George agreed to take it. What if he gave him the USB drive and the book?"

"Instead of it falling out of his pocket when he slipped on the ice?"

"Again, Drew slipping on the ice is George's story," Michael said delicately.

"Maybe that's where George went," suggested Olivia. "Maybe he went to the Bernstein party. Maybe he was trying to help Drew."

"Yes," said Ellie, "but Ryan said he didn't see George at the party."

"That doesn't mean he wasn't there. Don't the Bernsteins have a guardhouse? I'm guessing you can't just saunter on their property."

Olivia and Ellie nodded in unison. "We've catered there a couple times—we always had to be cleared at the gate."

"Perfect," said Michael, throwing a ten onto the counter. "Then let's see if we can retrace his steps."

"Five ninety-seven," said the clerk, swooping the bill from the counter.

"Keep the change," smiled Michael.

"Thank you!" gushed the cashier. "Merry Christmas."

"Merry Christmas," the trio chorused as they exited, although none of them were feeling very merry.

Ellie gunned the engine, flicked on the heat and seat warmers and maneuvered the car onto A1A, the main two-lane highway that ran parallel to the ocean.

"Where is the Bernstein estate?" Michael asked. "I've never been."

"Lantern Drive," Ellie replied, turning onto Sandy Pond Lane.

Michael stared out the window in silence. The houses grew from elegant homes to modest mansions, to sprawling oceanfront compounds. Ellie made a left onto Lantern Drive and came to a stop at a stone driveway. A brick guardhouse stood outside a set of ornate iron gates. Ellie slowly pulled into the drive and stopped at the gates.

A young man in a puffy yellow coat and black stocking cap stepped from the guardhouse, his expression polite but stern. "May I help you?"

"Yes, please. I'm Ellie Banks, owner of the Bitter Sweet Café."

"Yes…?" he prompted. "We don't have any deliveries scheduled for tonight."

"I'm not here for a delivery." The guard gave her a wary look. "We're trying to locate an older gentleman, who… let's say, is in a delicate mental state. His name is George Owens—he was supposed to be here playing Santa."

The young man rolled his eyes. "Delicate mental state is putting it lightly. He was here, but he was denied entrance. The Bernsteins have him on the no-admittance list, for obvious reasons."

"So, he wasn't allowed into the party?"

"Absolutely not," the young man replied curtly. "No admittance is pretty self-explanatory."

Any other time, Ellie would have given the young man a piece of her mind, but she needed information. Her eyes lowered to the name tag on the guard's puffy yellow jacket. "Mark, is there anything you can tell us? It's Christmas, and we just want to make sure he gets the help he needs. What time he was here? Which way he went when he left?"

Mark closed his eyes and took a deep breath, as if it took every ounce of willpower to continue. "After Mr. Owens was denied admittance, he tried to climb over the wall. As you can see, we have security everywhere." He gestured to a bank of cameras surrounding the guardhouse and others positioned along the wall. "I warned him that he was trespassing, and if he didn't leave immediately, I was going to call the police. Then he started going crazy, saying he had to deliver something to Giovanni Bono—he said it was life or death. I tried to calm him down, but he kept insisting that I let him in. I didn't have any choice but to call the police, and he bolted."

Michael looked at Ellie, his hunch had been right.

"Was Giovanni Bono at the party?" asked Ellie.

"I'm sorry, ma'am, but I can't tell you. That attendee list is kept private."

"I understand," Ellie smiled. "You've been very helpful."

"Have a nice evening," said Mark as Ellie put the car into reverse.

"Wait! One more question!"

"Ah," Ellie screeched, slamming on the breaks, causing the car to lurch. She turned and gave Michael a scathing look.

"Sorry, Ellie," he apologized. He fought with his seatbelt for a minute and leaned out the car window. "Mark, what time did you call the police?"

"Just a moment." The man let out another puffy sigh and disappeared into the guardhouse. He returned a moment later with his phone. "I called the police at eight-oh-seven."

"Thank you so much. We'll get out of your hair now," Michael smiled.

"Good luck." He watched as Ellie backed onto Lantern Avenue and then retreated into his guardhouse.

"You should never say, 'We'll get out of your hair' to a man with a hat," said Olivia. "He may be bald."

"I'll take my chances."

"Where to now?" Ellie asked. She turned onto Sandy Pond Lane heading back toward A1A.

Michael looked from Ellie to Olivia. "I think we all know where George is heading."

Ellie nodded. "Giovanni Bono's house."

Everyone knew that the Bono family was corrupt. Even though they claimed their family had ended their dealings with the Mafioso decades ago—there were rumors that they were still very much entrenched in illegal activities.

"Are you sure, Ellie? Giovanni isn't someone to be toyed with," reasoned Olivia. "There's a lot of rumors about what happens to people that get involved with him."

"I know," Ellie nodded. "I'm not afraid of him. What about you?" Ellie turned to face Michael, "You're unusually quiet."

"Sorry," said Michael, "I'm trying to put the pieces together."

"What have you got so far?" asked Olivia.

"Drew is dead."

Olivia made a disappointed face. "I hope there's more."

"If this were a football game, Drew was bound to lose in the end. He had one play, and he used it over and over."

"Blackmail," said Ellie.

"Exactly. And blackmail comes in all shapes and sizes. And it was effective when he used it on people like Ed and Tony. The threat of being exposed led them to do Drew's bidding."

"Right," Ellie agreed. "And if something works consistently, why deviate? It makes sense."

"Until it doesn't. Routines are why people get killed—not expecting the unexpected. Being overly confident is what gets people killed."

"Or robbed, like in Margaret's case," offered Olivia.

"We know that Drew's girlfriend stole the keycard so he could get into the Bono estate. I'm guessing that Drew took the black book, figuring he could use the contents as leverage against Giovanni."

"But something made him have a change of heart. Something that didn't fit into his typical blackmail formula," suggested Ellie.

"Exactly. Drew realizes that Giovanni knows he has the book, and instead of cowering, he sends some of his goons after him. Perhaps Drew offers to give the book back, but it's too late. He's already seen what's inside. No matter what choice he makes, he's a dead man."

"So you think it was one of Giovanni's goons that killed Drew?" asked Ellie.

"I do, and they're trying to frame the murder on George. I think Drew gave George the book at Schooners. I think Drew tried to run, to get out of town, but they caught him. Unfortunately, Drew no longer has the book. He's scared and tries to reason with them. He tells them that George has the book. They shoot him and he takes a swan dive onto the sleigh in George's front yard."

"Which leaves George in the same position as Drew. Giovanni doesn't know what he's seen, or if he took pictures of the contents…. If we can't find him, George is as good as dead," Ellie whispered.

"We need to find George as quickly as possible," insisted Michael.

Ellie flicked the blinker and eased onto Lighthouse Lane. Her headlights illuminated a triangular yellow sign that read *dead end*.

"That's an understatement," said Michael.

Dried leaves and ice crunched beneath her tires as she slowed the car to a crawl. Up ahead, the Bono estate looked like a miniature city—its occupant secured behind a ten-foot stone wall.

"I don't think it's a good idea to pull right up to his house," said Olivia.

"I have to agree with Olivia," Michael said, staring out the passenger-side window. "We should probably check things out on foot."

Ellie nodded, cut the engine, and flicked off the lights. Like the Bernstein estate, the Bono mansion drive led to an ornate wrought-iron gate the railing tipped with icy spear-pointed railheads. Decorative lanterns led from the entranceway, disappearing down the winding drive to the mansion.

"The Bonos and Bernsteins must shop at the same gate shop," Michael whispered.

"What now? Do we just go up to the gate like we did at the Bernsteins?" asked Olivia.

"What other choice do we have?" Ellie replied.

"We could go back to my house and drink cocoa and sit by the fire," Michael suggested. He was saved from Ellie's wrath when a woman's voice called out to them from the darkness.

"Excuse me!"

The trio spun in unison. A young woman was standing along the side of the road, dressed in baby blue boots, scrub pants and a huge puffy white coat that made her appear as if someone had stuffed her into a tower of powdered donuts. She brushed her hair away from her face with a gloved hand.

Michael clutched at his chest. "Good God, lady, you almost killed me." A small dog resembling a furry snowball sniffed his shoe and then lifted its rear leg, preparing to do its worst.

"Dudley!" the woman gasped. "Mind your manners." Dudley gave Michael a, you-got-lucky-this-time look, and then pranced away to join his owner. "I'm sorry about that. Dudley's learning boundaries."

"It's fine, I used to do the same thing. More of a territorial thing, not so much dealing with boundaries."

The woman arched an eyebrow and turned to Ellie and Olivia. "Not that it's any of my business but… are you guys lost?" the young woman asked.

"No," smiled Ellie, "we're just—"

"Just a simple, friendly word of caution," the woman interrupted. "I wouldn't go snooping around if I were you."

"We're not here to snoop," Ellie gave the woman a tight smile, "we're actually trying to track down my grandfather."

"Here? You do realize that's the Bono residence?" The woman scooped up Dudley, who immediately began giving her cold wet kisses.

"Yes, it's a long story. My grandfather is a professional Santa. People hire him to play Santa at their parties. He's not answering his phone or texts and… the Bono house was the last job he had on his calendar."

"He's getting old," Olivia added. "We didn't see his car and we were just worried about him."

"Dudley and I did see a man that looked a lot like Santa. Does he drive a…" the woman balled up her face. "Actually, I have no idea what kind of car it is—"

"A red car with wood paneling and a reindeer on the hood?" Ellie asked anxiously.

"Yes, that's it. He left a couple minutes before you got here, with two other people. A woman who looked to be about my age and a man."

"Thank you! You've been a huge help."

"You're welcome. Merry Christmas." The woman grabbed Dudley's paw and waved bye to the trio as they raced toward Ellie's car.

Michael barely had enough time to close the door before Ellie smashed on the gas, spinning the car around, spitting snow.

"The only way out of here is Seaside Lane—it connects to A1A," said Michael, looking at his phone. The car fishtailed and then picked up speed.

"If they get to A1A we'll never catch them," warned Olivia.

"Actually, if they go North, they'll be heading back toward town."

"Which means more police, and more visibility," Olivia declared.

"Not to mention that his car stands out like a sore thumb." Ellie slid to a stop at the intersection of Seaside and A1A and turned South onto the empty highway. Brightly lit condos and homes peppered the landscape, each fighting for their little slice of sand and a view of the ocean.

"Tail lights," Michael blurted, jabbing his finger at the windshield.

"I see them," said Elie.

"Don't get too close, we don't want whoever's with George to make any rash decisions."

The words had barely left Michael's lips when the brake lights on George's car flashed, and then disappeared.

"Isn't that the Atlantic Pier up ahead?" Ellie nodded, pressing her foot on the brakes. "Hit the lights so they don't see us," suggested Michael.

Ellie flicked off the headlights and cautiously eased her car around the corner. George's car was parked in front of the wooden stairwell that led to the pier.

"Park behind the dumpster," said Michael. A gust of wind whipped up the narrow roadway, peppering the car with sand.

The trio exited the car and were immediately assaulted by the disgusting smell of rotting fish and garbage coming from the dumpster. In the distance, three silhouettes walked toward the end of the pier. The glint of metal flashed in the hand of the man in the rear of the group.

"It's George and Drew's girlfriend." Ellie whispered, putting her hand over her mouth.

"We need to get to that shed," Michael said. "It's where they keep rental rods and equipment. We may find something we can use."

"Like what? A life vest?" asked Olivia.

"I'm not sure," Michael replied. "I'm formulating a plan as I go."

"God help us," Ellie moaned, following him through the shadows to the supply shed.

Michael peeked around the corner. Just as the man with the gun and his hostages reached the top of the stairs. He gave George a vicious shove, sending him face forward onto the pier. "Get up!" the man snarled.

Anger surged through Michael as the man grabbed the back of George's jacket and hauled him to his feet. Michael crawled back to Ellie and Olivia. "Ellie, call the police. I'm going to do something stupid."

"That's your plan? Michael!" She reached out to grab his arm, but he shrugged away.

Michael slipped around the corner, hoping the crashing of the waves and the wind would cover the sound of what he was about to do. He took several steps back and ran, hurling his body into the wooden doors. There was a loud crunching sound. Not the door, but his shoulder. He bounced backward, landing with a heavy thud.

"Are you okay?" Ellie peered around the corner at him. Michael waved her off and climbed back to his feet. "Did you try the doorknob?"

"Do you think I'm an idiot?"

"Please don't make me answer that," said Ellie.

Michael grasped the knob in his hand and twisted, the door swung open. "I must have jarred it loose." He disappeared inside and emerged seconds later, brandishing a wooden oar.

Michael reached the top of the stairs and knelt. A gust of frigid wind whipped along the pier. He froze in his tracks. He could see George's attacker much clearer now. He was dressed in black sweat pants and a black hoodie, which the wind kept flipping off his head. George and Drew's girlfriend had the backs to the railing at the end of the pier.

The attacker reached his hand into his pocket and handed George a cell phone. "Turn it on," he grunted. George clumsily fumbled with the phone. "Hurry!" snarled the man.

Michael could see a flash of light as the phone booted up. The man waited a moment, snatched the phone from George and flung it into the ocean.

"You look confused, old man," he mocked him. "You see, your cell phone will ping the closest tower. So after you kill her and push her into the ocean, the police will know you were here. Plus, the red fiber from your ridiculous little suit on the pole over there, and Drew's blood in your car is *all* the evidence the police are going to need." The man put his gun to George's head. "You're going to be so upset after killing her, that you decide to kill yourself as well."

"I'll never shoot her!" George cried out.

"Oh but you will, I need your fingerprints on the gun. You might as well cooperate, either way, she's going to die."

George looked over at the young woman, tears streamed from her eyes. Her hair clung to her lips and cheeks. "I'm sorry," she whispered.

"How touching," laughed the man. He grabbed George and spun him around so that he was behind him. He put the gun in George's hand and grabbed his wrist. "You're doing great, Santa." He raised George's hand, aligning the gun so it was even with the woman's chest. "Good, now, all you've got to do is pull the trigger, and it will be over."

In the distance, a speedboat appeared, making its way across the ocean, heading toward the pier. The attacker turned his head for just a second, and that was when Michael slammed him in the back with a boat oar.

It all happened in an instant. The man fell forward against George. Who fired the gun, striking the woman in the shoulder. Surprise flashed in her eyes as she toppled backward off the pier into the ocean. Without a thought, George dived after her, into the churning, freezing ocean.

The man whirled on Michael—his eyes filled with rage. In his hand, he held a gleaming knife with a serrated edge, shark teeth, for tearing and ripping flesh.

"You're an idiot." The man smiled. "And now you're dead."

"Actually," Michael said, "you've got your tenses wrong. I'm still alive. It should be 'And now you're going to die.'"

The man's smile turned into a sickening sneer. He pivoted, twisting his body, and then hurled the knife at Michael's torso. There was a sickening thud. Michael felt the impact against his chest. He stumbled backward, teetering on the edge of the pier. *This is it.* He waited for the searing agony, for that painful last beat of his heart.

"Michael!"

Ellie's scream tore through the night, and that was when Michael realized he had somehow blocked the knife with his oar. The man in the hoodie charged, and for a split second, Michael was back on the ice in Boston, a teenager, playing hockey. He faked high and then brought the edge of the oar crashing into the man's knee.

He screamed in pain and fell to the ground, clutching his leg. Ellie rushed in, and Michael tossed the oar to her. Without hesitation, she smacked him across the back of the head, knocking him unconscious.

Olivia raced to the edge of the pier, scanning the water for George and the woman. Sirens wailed in the distance.

"There!" Ellie yelled, joining her.

George emerged from the water, stumbling to the shoreline, carrying the woman in his arms. A series of flashlights bobbed on the beach, heading toward George.

The black speedboat spun around in a tight U, throwing up a wall of water, and disappeared along the coastline, into the night.

Chapter 11

"And here we go, Ellie, a café latte with a dash of cinnamon," Michael said, putting a steaming cup of joe in front of her.

"Are you sure the coffee's good here? You know I am a bit of a coffee snob."

"Oh…," Michael snatched a napkin from the table and folded it across his arm. "My lady, here at the Bitter Sweet Café we serve only the finest brews. We source our beans from local farmers in Costa Rica and Brazil. I'm sure that you will find our coffee pleasing to even the most refined palate."

"Bravo! Bravo!" Olivia laughed. "You're hired. Get that man an apron."

Michael gave a slight bow. "Lady Olivia, you look stunning this morning. I bring to you a caramel macchiato with freshly whipped cream, and a handful of those tiny marshmallows."

"Gorgeous," Olivia whispered.

"Thank you," Michael replied. "I get that a lot. And, Sir George the Brave, a cup of our finest joe with a splash of cream and two squares of sugar."

"Thank you, Michael." George beamed up at him. "Masterfully done."

"Thank you." Michael flung the napkin from his arm with a flourish. "I shall return momentarily."

"I think someone finally got some sleep." George chuckled.

"I think so. It's been stressful for everyone these past few days," Ellie smiled.

"Did I miss anything?" Michael asked, sliding into his seat and sitting two cups of coffee on the table.

"Two cups, Michael?" Olivia stared at him, shaking her head. "Are things that bad?"

"I couldn't decide. There was pumpkin spice and then a cinnamon roast. I'm going to alternate sips. I believe William Cowper said it best, in his famous poem *The Task*. Variety is the very spice of life, that gives it all its flavor."

"Well, if it's in a poem," Ellie reasoned, "then it has to be true."

"Undeniably," Michael agreed.

"So, George," Ellie said. "I spoke to Officer Ryan this morning. He said that you're free and clear."

"Yes, thank you so much, Ellie." George beamed. "And thanks, you guys, too." He smiled at Olivia and Michael. "If it hadn't been for your help, things would have ended much differently."

"That's what friends are for. We've got each other's backs," smiled Michael.

"About that," said George, his cheeks reddening, "I'm terribly sorry about lying to all of you… I wanted to tell you the truth about the book, and I was. But when I went to your guestroom to call Gordon, my phone rang. It was Sarah—"

"I'm guessing Sarah was Drew's girlfriend?"

"Yes," George nodded. "She told me they were going to kill her if I didn't bring the book to the Bonos." He shook his head. "I knew that I just couldn't get you all involved. So I decided to continue hiding the book and lied about calling Gordon."

"It's okay, we understand," Ellie said, squeezing George's hand. "I would have done the same thing."

Michael and Olivia nodded in agreement.

"Now the one thing we've all been dying to know: Did you see what was in the book?" Michael asked.

"No! Sarah tried to tell me, but I told her I didn't want to know. She told me Drew stole it to try to get back into the good graces of the Calvetti crime family—but of course, it didn't work out that way."

"Do you think the police are going to investigate Mr. Bono?" Ellie asked. "I hear his family has been untouchable for generations."

"I don't know." George shook his head and clasped his weathered hands on the table. "Detective Mitchell thinks Mr. Bono will be well insulated from anything that happens. The Bonos are saying they have no idea who the man at the pier was, and that he acted on his own. Plus, witnesses at the Bernstein's party claim that Mr. Bono was there during the entire party."

"So you never saw Mr. Bono?" Ellie asked.

"No, only the man who tried to kill us."

"What's going to happen to Sarah?"

"I don't know…. She knows what's inside the book. Maybe she'll exchange information for a lighter sentence—maybe even witness protection, who knows?"

Ellie nodded, deep in thought. "I would definitely choose witness protection. If not, she'll be looking over her shoulders for the rest of her life."

Michael looked at his friends and shook his head. "Come on, guys, how about we change topics for a bit? We stopped a murder, broke up a crime ring, George is back to being Santa again and..." he pulled out three envelopes, "...I have a little Christmas gift for all of you."

George gave Michael a curious stare.

"I'll explain later. But for now...," Michael handed each of his friends an envelope.

"Twelve hundred and fifty dollars?!" Olivia gushed. "Michael, this is too much."

"It's not from me," he exclaimed, "it's from our mystery friend! He gave us five thousand dollars to make things right, and I'm dividing our reward equally."

"And you have no idea who this mystery man is?" Ellie asked.

"None. But he was adamant that I take the money."

"I don't deserve this." George slid his envelope back across the table.

"You deserve it more than any of us," Ellie said. "You protected your friends, risked your life to save Sarah, and you brought happiness and joy to the people of Lana Cove for—"

"Over a hundred years," laughed Michael.

George's face turned bright red. "Thank you, Ellie. Michael, you're getting coal again this year."

"Can you bring it in the shape of briquettes, I want to do more grilling this year."

Olivia's eyes widened and the smile disappeared from her face.

"What? My cooking isn't that bad…," Michael followed Olivia's gaze. "Oh."

George's picture appeared on the local news. The same newscaster who had stood in front of his house, now stood on the pier where just a few hours ago, George and his friends had battled for their lives.

Ellie glanced around the café warily. Everyone's attention was focused on the television. She wanted to jump from her seat and rip the cord from the wall, but she sat there, as if glued to her chair.

The news anchor's hair whipped around her face. She pulled up her collar on her coat to try to shield her microphone from the wind. "We're here at the scene where Gabriel Roccio was arrested for kidnapping and allegedly trying to murder Sarah Lewis and George Owens." The camera operator zoomed in on the anchorwoman.

"Police tell us that Sarah was shot in the shoulder, fell off the pier and that eighty-five-year-old George Owens dove in after her." In an encore performance, the cameraman zoomed in on the railing, and then down to the crashing waves some forty feet below.

"We have some eyewitness video of that rescue—we apologize for the quality." The television screen became jerky, obviously the person videoing was running.

"He's in the water! Help him!"

There were more shouts. The video swung up, showing crashing waves, and a group of people running to the shoreline as George marched through the surf, carrying a woman in his arms. A wave crashed over him, he disappeared below the surface and reemerged, fighting to keep Sarah's head out of the water.

"Thanks to George Owens's bravery and heroic actions, Sarah Lewis will be fine." The words *Lana Cove Hero* scrawled across the screen.

The Bitter Sweet Café was silent for a moment—the only sound was the drumbeat of *The Little Drummer Boy* and the news anchor wishing everyone a safe and Merry Christmas.

Suddenly, a man leaped to his feet and shouted, "George, George!" throwing his fist into the air.

Soon, the entire café was on their feet shouting, "George!"

Michael studied Ellie—it was wonderful to see her smiling again. She was beautiful—her brown eyes filled with joy. He pulled a card from his pocket and slid it across the table to her.

"What's this?" she asked. The outside of the card read: *Inside this card lies your secret desire.* "Oh, well," Ellie laughed, feeling her cheeks redden. "I'm not sure I want to look at this here."

"Go on!" Olivia exclaimed.

Ellie rolled her eyes and opened the envelope. A spring-loaded mistletoe branch shot up, hovering over her head.

She gazed at Michael and smiled. "Okay, you win."

"Yes!" Michael stood and leaned across the table, puckering his lips.

Ellie stared deep into his eyes and then turned and gave George a big kiss on the cheek. "Merry Christmas, George."

George's face turned bright red, and his nose glowed like Rudolph's. Michael's mouth fell open as he glanced from Ellie to George, then back to Ellie.

"Maybe next year," Olivia laughed, patting him on his back.

George looked adoringly at his friends and winked at Michael. "Best Christmas ever, best Christmas ever."

Thank you for reading *Sleighed*

Thank you so much for reading the first book in *The Coffee House Sleuths Christmas* series! We hope you loved the characters!

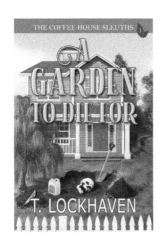

If you haven't read the main stories of *The Coffee House Sleuths*, you may start with *A Garden to Die For*, the first book in this cozy mystery series. Find out what happens when Michael moves from Boston, Massachusetts to Lana Cove, North Carolina and finds a finger in the front yard of his newly purchased home.

Order *A Garden to Die For* now so you don't miss out!

Others by T. Lockhaven

If you enjoyed *Sleighed*, then you may enjoy T. Lockhaven's witch cozy mystery series. Check out *Merry and Moody Witch Cozy Mysteries: Potion Commotion*. A young witch returns home to find her family missing, a dead body and the police have her in their crosshairs as the prime suspect.

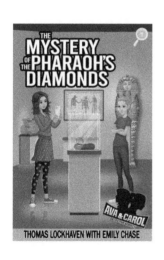

If you're looking for a mystery series for girls ages 8-12, T. Lockhaven writes the *Ava & Carol Detective Agency* series under the author name Thomas Lockhaven.

"For every girl who wants to be Nancy Drew or Stephanie Plum." Buckle up and start this thrilling Ava and Carol detective series enjoyed by thousands of middle schoolers today. *The Mystery of the Pharaoh's Diamonds* is the first of many in the series.

We appreciate your help in spreading the word, including telling a friend. Reviews help readers find books! Please leave a review on your favorite book site!

Sign up for our newsletter to find out about new books: twistedkeypublishing.com